Princess
in Disguise

Also by E. D. Baker

THE TALES OF THE FROG PRINCESS:

The Frog Princess

Dragon's Breath

Once Upon a Curse

No Place for Magic

The Salamander Spell

The Dragon Princess

Dragon Kiss

A Prince among Frogs

———•———

Fairy Wings

Fairy Lies

———•———

TALES OF THE WIDE-AWAKE PRINCESS:

The Wide-Awake Princess

Unlocking the Spell

The Bravest Princess

———•———

A Question of Magic

———•———

The Fairy-Tale Matchmaker

A Tale of the Wide-Awake Princess

Princess in Disguise

E. D. BAKER

BLOOMSBURY

NEW YORK   LONDON   NEW DELHI   SYDNEY

First published in the United States of America in March 2015
by Bloomsbury Children's Books
www.bloomsbury.com

Bloomsbury is a registered trademark of Bloomsbury Publishing Plc

For information about permission to reproduce selections from this book, write to
Permissions, Bloomsbury Children's Books, 1385 Broadway, New York, New York 10018
Bloomsbury books may be purchased for business or promotional use.
For information on bulk purchases please contact Macmillan Corporate and
Premium Sales Department at specialmarkets@macmillan.com

Library of Congress Cataloging-in-Publication Data
Baker, E. D.
Princess in disguise / by E. D. Baker.
      pages   cm
Summary: When everything starts going wrong on Annie and Liam's wedding
day, Queen Karolina decides that they need the help of her fairy godmother,
Moonbeam, but a magical fog keeps messengers from leaving so Annie and
Liam themselves set out to discover who ruined the wedding, and why.
ISBN 978-1-61963-573-9 (hardcover) • ISBN 978-1-61963-574-6 (e-book)
[1. Fairy tales. 2. Princesses—Fiction. 3. Magic—Fiction. 4. Disguise—Fiction.
5. Weddings—Fiction. 6. Characters in literature—Fiction.] I. Title.
PZ8.B173Pt 2015   [Fic]—dc23   2014024657

Book design by Donna Mark
Typeset by Newgen Knowledge Works (P) Ltd., Chennai, India
Printed and bound in the U.S.A. by Thomson-Shore Inc., Dexter, Michigan
2 4 6 8 10 9 7 5 3 1

All papers used by Bloomsbury Publishing, Inc., are natural, recyclable products
made from wood grown in well-managed forests. The manufacturing processes
conform to the environmental regulations of the country of origin.

This book is dedicated to Victoria Wells Arms, for her insight and guidance; to Brett Wright, who keeps me on track; to Kim, my research assistant and mapmaker; to Ellie, for her secretarial skills; to Kevin, my techno-wizard; and to my fans, who keep asking for more.

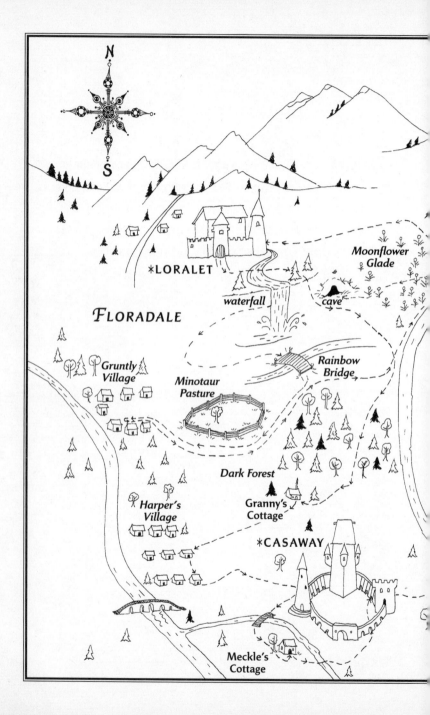

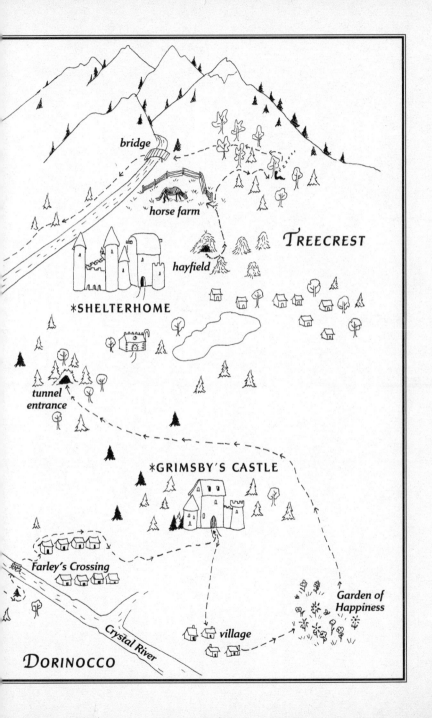

CHAPTER 1

"I KNOW SOMETHING YOU DON'T KNOW!" an eerie voice whispered in a singsong way.

Annie's eyes shot open and she stared into the dark, trying to see if someone was in the room with her. Enough moonlight came through the window that she could see that her bedchamber was empty. When she spotted the disembodied head that seemed to be floating in the corner, her heart lurched. It took her a moment to recognize the face in the magic mirror. She'd had the mirror moved to the far corner only the day before and wasn't used to seeing it there.

"Oh, it's you," Annie mumbled, and snuggled deeper under her covers. "Unless the castle is about to fall down around our ears, I don't want to hear about it. I'm getting married tomorrow and I need my rest. Don't wake me again until morning."

"Well, if that's the way you're going to be!" the mirror declared in a huff. "I won't tell you even if you beg me to."

"Beg you to what?" Annie murmured, nearly asleep again.

"I'm not saying," replied the mirror, but Annie didn't hear.

❦

She woke the next morning with the nagging feeling that the mirror had something important to say the night before. For a moment she thought about getting up and asking it, but there was a knock on the door and Lilah peeked in.

"Are you awake?" Lilah asked.

"Just barely," Annie told her, brushing her hair back from her face. "You're up early."

"And you should be, too," said Lilah as she opened the door the rest of the way. She came in bearing a tray, and used her foot to push the door closed behind her. "I thought you might like some breakfast before you're too busy to eat."

"How thoughtful!" Annie said. "But it looks as if you've brought enough for two. Would you like to join me?"

"I was hoping you'd ask," Lilah said with a grin.

While Annie sat up and plumped the pillows behind her, Lilah carried the tray over and set it on the bed. Hiking her skirts up to her knees, she climbed onto the high mattress and reached for a biscuit.

Although everyone else thought Lilah was a servant girl, Annie knew the truth. Lilah was a runaway princess who had been hiding in Snow White's castle when Annie found and befriended her. Before Annie had brought her to Treecrest, Lilah had dressed in dirty clothes and smelly furs, hoping to hide her identity. Annie had made her bathe and wear nicer clothes, although Lilah insisted that she still had to hide among the servants.

"Are you sure I can't convince you to change your mind about coming to the wedding?" asked Annie before taking a sip of cider.

"The servants won't be there, and I don't want to stand out in any way. You've done so much for me, and I'll be forever grateful, but I still have to be careful. If anyone recognizes me and word gets back to my father, I'll have to run again. Now that I no longer look like a drudge, I worry that someone is going to recognize me every time someone new comes to the castle. When that silk merchant came from Westerling a few weeks ago, he stared at me so long and hard that I was certain he knew who I was."

"But he didn't say anything to you, did he?" said Annie. "I'm sure you imagined it."

Lilah shrugged. "Maybe, but I still don't want to do anything that will make me stand out."

"If you insist," said Annie. "Here, have another biscuit. You're too thin for your own good. I think you should—"

Suddenly the door popped open and a figure no taller than Annie's knee skipped into the room. Seeing Lilah, he scratched his head and said, "I don't know much about human customs, but why is a servant sitting on your bed, Princess?"

Lilah scooted off the bed, nearly knocking over the tray.

"I dropped something and she was helping me look for it," said Annie.

"In your bed?" said the sprite. "Were you looking at your ladybug collection? Or do you collect pretty stones? I collect both and sometimes I sort them while I'm in bed. One time I lost some of my bugs in my bed and couldn't find them for weeks. Of course, my mattress is made of moss and—"

"Your Highness, if you are finished with your breakfast, I can take the tray for you," Lilah said, looking flustered.

"Breakfast!" the little sprite said, his eyes lighting up. "I already ate in the great hall, but I could find room for more if you can spare it."

He looked at the tray so longingly that Annie had to laugh. "Go ahead and help yourself, Squidge." Glancing at the door as Lilah closed it behind her, she sighed. There was so much she'd like to do for her, if only the girl would let her.

"Mmm," the sprite said as he swallowed a bite of biscuit. "Yours are even better than the ones downstairs."

4

Annie smiled. She had met the little sprite while looking for the dwarf who had turned Gwendolyn's beloved Beldegard into a bear. They had stopped at the Moonflower Glade to talk to the fairy Moonbeam, and met her assistant, Squidge, instead. Shortly after Annie and Liam announced their wedding date, the sprite had arrived at the castle, explaining that Moonbeam was busy with her new husband and didn't need Squidge's help just then. Annie was happy to accept his offer to assist with the wedding. He had proven to be very helpful, and Annie had remarked more than once that he was a lot nicer than he had seemed in the Moonflower Glade.

Taking another biscuit, Squidge slathered jam all over it and crammed the whole thing into his mouth. He chewed it with his eyes half-closed, then glanced at Annie and said, "Why aren't you dressed already? You're not canceling the wedding, are you?"

Crumbs shot out of his mouth as he talked, landing on the coverlet. Annie moved her plate out of the way. "I would get up and get dressed if you'd leave."

"In a minute," said Squidge. He ate two more biscuits, gulping them down without really chewing. "As I told you before, I wanted to help with your wedding to thank you for introducing Moonbeam to her new husband. If it weren't for you, they wouldn't have fallen in love and gotten married. I've never seen Moonbeam so happy." He made a sour face, but when he caught Annie looking at him, it turned into a smile.

"I hope you like everything I've done. I want you and Liam to have the kind of wedding you deserve. I know you've been busy, but I did what you asked me to, plus lots more. I washed all the dogs that live in the castle, I weeded the courtyard, I scrubbed the dungeon steps, I took care of the invitations, I polished the spires on the towers, I entertained the visiting children, and watered the garden every day. Say, are you going to eat that biscuit?" He licked his lips as he pointed at the one on her plate.

"Yes," she said, and picked it up. "I really do appreciate all that you've done for us." She took a bite, even though Squidge was staring at her mouth as she did it.

"Apparently not enough to give me that biscuit," he grumbled under his breath. "Anyway, I came to ask if there's anything else you need me to do. I could polish the floor in the great hall or give baths to all the cats. The weather is going to be beautiful today, so the cats would dry fast."

"That won't be necessary," said Annie. "My wedding guests would slip if the floor was polished now, and the cats would all be in very bad moods."

There was a knock on the door and her friend Snow White called out, "May we come in?"

"Of course," Annie called back.

The door opened, admitting Snow White and Eleanor, a lovely young woman who had just married Annie's cousin, Ainsley. The two girls were already dressed for Annie's wedding, and a cloud of perfume entered the room with them. Squidge raised his head to sniff the air. With his face scrunched up as if he'd smelled something bad, he hopped off the bed. "Gotta go," he said. "Lots to do."

Annie hardly noticed as he scurried out the door, because Snow White was already talking. "We came to see if you need help with anything."

"Not really," said Annie. "I think everything is under control."

"We could help with your dress or your hair," offered Eleanor.

Annie shook her head. "Thank you, Eleanor, but my mother wants me to come to her chamber to get dressed."

"Oh, please don't call me Eleanor. Call me Ella like my father did. Eleanor reminds me of my stepmother. She used to call me Eleanor before she started calling me Cinderella. That goes for you, too, Snow White. I want all my friends to call me Ella."

"Then we will, Ella," Annie said with a smile.

"We wanted to tell you how happy we are for you, Annie," Snow White told her. "Liam is perfect for you. He's wonderful and loves you so much. After seeing you two together, I knew that I wanted a husband just like him. He's what inspired me to choose Maitland—a good man who loves me for myself."

"That's how I feel about Ainsley," said Ella.

Squidge hadn't closed the door all the way when he left, and now it opened wide as Annie's sister, Gwendolyn, walked in. "Oh good, you're awake," she said, seeing Annie sitting up in bed. "I came to see if you had any questions for your older, already married sister."

Gwennie and her new husband, Beldegard, had returned from their grand tour only two days before, giving the sisters little time to talk.

"You've been married for just over a month," said Annie.

"Yes," Gwennie said as she plunked herself on the edge of the bed. "But I've learned so much about men that I never knew! What would you like to ask me?"

"Uh, nothing?" said Annie.

"Well, I have a question," said Snow White. "I'm getting married soon, but before I do, there is one thing I've been wondering and I didn't know who to ask. It's very personal, but I couldn't talk to my father about it and I don't have a mother to ask."

"What is it? I'll be happy to talk about anything!" said Gwennie.

"Do all men snore? The dwarves all did and it made a horrible racket at night. I was always glad that my room was on a different floor and I could shut the door at night."

"Snoring? That's what you want to ask me? I thought you wanted to know about . . ." Gwennie gasped as her gaze landed on the magic mirror in the corner. "I heard you had a magic mirror in your room, but I didn't know it was so big!" she told Annie. "I have *got* to ask it a question!"

Snow White glanced at the mirror with distaste. "You can, but I'm not going near it. That thing reminds me of my evil stepmother."

"That's all right," said Gwennie. "I have plenty of questions for it. Let's see, which one should I ask first? Ah, I know. Mirror, mirror, on the wall, how many children will I have?"

"That doesn't rhyme," said Ella. "I thought the questions you asked magic mirrors always had to rhyme."

"Rhyming isn't necessary," said Annie as she watched mist begin to form in the mirror.

When the face appeared in the swirling mist, it looked annoyed. "What do I look like—a crystal ball? I can't predict the future!"

"Well then," said Gwennie. "Tell me this. Who is the handsomest prince of all?" She looked smug as she waited for the answer, and surprised when the image of a blindingly handsome prince wearing a cape of blue-striped skins appeared.

"That would be Prince Larsenvarsen from the kingdom of Skol," said the mirror.

Irritation came through in Gwennie's voice when she said, "Let me rephrase that. Who is the handsomest formerly enchanted prince?"

"Prince Cumberpants of Grimswald," the mirror said as two images appeared side by side. One was a frog looking very unhappy. The other was a handsome prince wearing a goofy grin.

"Uh, Gwennie, you can't ask it too many questions," Annie told her. "The mirror is going to run out of power soon."

"I know, I know!" Gwennie replied. "I just want to hear the mirror say his name. Who is the handsomest formerly enchanted prince who was once a bear?"

"Prince Allyoop from Skreevakia." The image of a cuddly little bear cub appeared beside that of a handsome dark-haired child, but the picture was fainter than before.

"This is ridiculous!" cried Gwennie. "Why can't this mirror give me the right answer?"

"Gwennie, you really can't—" Annie began.

"Just one more," said her sister. "Mirror, who is the handsomest formerly enchanted prince who was once a very big bear whose name begins with 'B' and ends in 'ard'?"

"That would be Prince Beldegard, although Prince Borisigard is a close second," the mirror said, showing two images that were so faint that they were almost impossible to see.

"Finally!" cried Gwennie. "Annie, this mirror is defective. You should get rid of it."

The face was gone, but the swirling mist was still there. Suddenly, bright lights flickered in the mist, then the whole thing went black.

"I think you upset it," Annie said. "I'm sorry, ladies, but I'm going to have to ask you to leave so I can get dressed. I'll talk to all of you after the wedding."

"We're leaving," said Gwennie. "I almost wish I had come home sooner so I could have helped you plan your wedding. If it were my wedding, I would have done things very differently. Why, I was telling Beldegard that you really should have—"

"I'll talk to you later, Gwennie. Thanks for stopping by, everyone!" Annie said, shooing the princesses out of the room and shutting the door. Hearing Gwennie talk had reminded Annie of what her sister had been like when she married Beldegard. She had been demanding, overly sensitive, and so concerned with what she wanted that she had made everyone else's lives miserable. Annie couldn't stand being around her sister then, and was determined not to act the way her sister had or treat anyone the way Gwennie had treated her.

CHAPTER 2

QUEEN KAROLINA HAD MADE IT very clear that Annie was to come straight to see her the moment she got out of bed. As Annie hurried along the corridor, she glanced to the far end, where a window revealed a beautiful cloudless day, just as Squidge had said. It was the perfect kind of day for a wedding.

The little sprite wasn't the only one who had offered to help. Annie's aunt and uncle, Queen Theodora and King Daneel, were there, as well as their son, Prince Ainsley, and his new wife. Ella had been an enormous help with the more practical matters like seating arrangements at the formal dinner and choosing the food to be served after the ceremony. Snow White and her betrothed, Prince Maitland, had arrived a day later, even though they were in the midst of their own wedding preparations. Snow White had hit it off with Ella right away and together they had taken over decorating the castle. With Squidge and Annie's friends to help, Annie had little left to do, other than get dressed and calm her mother's nerves.

Her mother had been agitated since the day Annie and Liam returned from helping Snow White and announced that they planned to marry right away. Queen Karolina had just finished putting on a wedding for her older daughter, Gwendolyn, and hadn't expected Annie's announcement quite so soon. When Liam said that he wanted to marry Annie that week, the queen announced that no daughter of hers was going to get married in anything but the most beautiful ceremony, and that would take at least two months. They were able to talk her down to one, but that had only been after much wheedling, begging, and threats of elopement. Everyone in the castle had worked overtime to get things ready, but Annie's gown hadn't been finished when she went to bed the night before.

Annie and Liam had thought long and hard about their invitation list, and had finally decided that they had to invite all the witches and fairies in the kingdom if they wanted to stay on cordial terms with them. Although there weren't very many witches in Treecrest, there were lots of fairies. None had arrived yet, but Annie was sure that they planned to make a big entrance, arriving together just before the wedding. More worrisome, however, was that Liam's father had yet to arrive. They had invited him as soon as they set the date and had welcomed a messenger bearing a reply soon after. He had promised to come, but there was still no sign of the elderly king. Annie wondered if she should once again offer to postpone the wedding, an offer she had already made to Liam the day before. He had turned her down then, saying that he expected his father to show up any minute.

"There you are!" Lady Clare exclaimed as she rushed down the corridor to take Annie by the arm. "Your mother has been waiting for you!"

Annie let the woman lead her into the queen's chamber. Although it was a large room, it seemed small with all the ladies-in-waiting there along with the two seamstresses who were still fussing over the gowns they had made for Annie and her mother.

Queen Karolina turned away from her mirror to glare at Annie. "It's about time! Where have you been?"

"I came straight here," Annie replied. "Did Liam's father arrive yet?"

"No, but I'm sure he's on his way. The ceremony isn't due to start for another three hours," said the queen.

"What if he doesn't get here in time? Maybe we should postpone it until—"

"You will do no such thing!" her mother cried. "You bullied me into having the wedding today and you're not going to change it now. I've worked my fingers to the bone trying to make this perfect. Nothing is going to make us postpone this wedding!"

Annie could tell that her mother was annoyed with her, but she was too worried to give up. "He should be here by now. What if something has gone wrong?"

The queen sighed as if it was all too much. "If something had gone wrong and he wasn't able to come, he would have sent word. Now please, go look at your dress. Mabel and Inga just finished it."

The two seamstresses bobbed their heads, beaming at Annie, but she could see the shadows under their eyes and knew they had been up all night. Her mother wasn't the only one who had put a lot of work into the wedding. Maybe it wouldn't be fair to any of them if she postponed it now.

Lady Clare had already crossed the room to where the seamstresses hovered over the gown. "It's gorgeous!" she exclaimed. "Oh, dear, there's a loose thread."

The moment Lady Clare touched the thread, Annie heard twanging as if someone had struck a harsh chord on a lute. "No, don't!" Annie cried out, but the magic she'd heard had already done its work. At the touch of the woman's hand, every thread in the gown came undone and the fabric fluttered to the floor in scraps, while all the hand-sewn pearls and gems fell with a loud clatter.

Queen Karolina gasped and turned pale. Lady Clare's hand flew to her mouth and she shook her head. "I barely touched it!" she cried, turning to the queen.

"It wasn't your fault," said Annie, although her heart was sinking. The gown had been the one she had always

15

envisioned herself wearing at her wedding. It had been perfect, and now it was destroyed. Even though all the pieces were there, it would be weeks before the dress could be remade. "Someone used magic to ruin my wedding gown. I could hear it!"

No one seemed to think this was odd, as they all knew that Annie actually could hear magic. Because of the first and only christening gift she had received from a fairy, Annie was impervious to magic, but she always knew when it was present.

"Why would anyone do such an awful thing?" the queen asked.

"I don't know," said Annie with a catch in her voice. "I mean, I know I've made enemies, but I've already dealt with Terobella and Granny Bentbone. I didn't know anyone else hated me enough to do something like this."

Granny Bentbone and her daughter, Terobella, were evil witches whom Annie had defeated while visiting Snow White. Terobella had destroyed herself when she tried to use magic on Annie, and Granny Bentbone was currently locked away in a tower under armed guard. After dealing with the witches, Annie had accepted Liam's proposal on the way home, certain that no one else wished her ill the way they had. She'd thought that her only worry now was that she didn't become the same demanding, imperious, self-centered harridan that her sister, Gwendolyn, had been when she had been about to get married. Remembering her resolve to be considerate of others' feelings even if things didn't go quite the way she wanted them to, she tried not to let her disappointment over her ruined gown show.

The queen must have noticed the unshed tears glistening in Annie's eyes, because her own expression softened. "Oh, my poor darling. Don't worry. I'm sure we'll think of some way around this. Perhaps I have a gown we could alter. Lady Clare, see what you can find that might work. Lady Suzette, empty out that jeweled box and help the seamstresses collect all the pearls and gems. We have a lot to do and only a few hours to do it."

Boom! Thunder shook the room as lightning flashed close by. Everyone turned to the window when rain began to pour from the sky. What had been a beautiful day just minutes before was suddenly dark and stormy.

In the silence between rumbles of thunder, they all heard a knock on the door. One of the ladies-in-waiting opened it to admit a maid. "Your Highness," she said, looking around the room until she spotted Annie. "You need to come quick. It's the two princesses Snow White and Eleanor. Something terrible has happened to them!"

"Was there an accident?" asked Queen Karolina.

"Are they ill?" asked Annie.

"No, no! It's worse than that," cried the maid. "They have rashes!"

Everyone looked confused, but it was Annie who spoke up first. "Excuse me, Mother. I should go see about this," she said, curtsying to the queen.

"Of course, my dear. You take care of your friends and we'll see to a gown for you." The queen looked relieved that she wouldn't have to deal with this newest emergency.

The maid was so upset that she nearly tripped over her own feet as they ran down the corridor. "Where are they?" Annie asked.

"In Princess Eleanor's room," said the maid. "I was brushing her hair when Princess Snow White came by. They were both fine, then suddenly they claimed to be hot and I looked at their faces and . . . Well, you'll see for yourself. They're in here."

Annie led the way into the room, stopping so suddenly that the maid bumped into her from behind. The two princesses were seated in chairs in front of the window, gazing at each other in bewilderment. They had rashes, but they weren't like any that Annie had ever seen before. Bright green splotches moved across their faces, drifting from chin to cheek to forehead and back again, making one pattern after another.

"Creeping rashes?" Annie murmured out loud.

"Is that what they're called?" asked Snow White. "Then you've seen them before?"

Annie shook her head. "No. Never. But they have to have been magically induced. Nothing that looks like that could be natural. Just a moment and we'll know for sure." Annie approached her friends with her hand outstretched. At her touch, the rash disappeared from Snow White's fair skin, reappearing when Annie took her hand away. "It's magic all right. Aside from holding your hands, there's nothing I can do about it."

"Has anyone seen Annie?" Liam asked as he stuck his head in the still-open door. "I just . . . Oh, there you are. You're needed in the great hall. Something about the rushes and the flowers. Say, what happened to you two?"

Liam was staring at the two princesses when they both burst into tears. Annie sighed and hustled her groom out the door, closing it firmly behind her. "What is this about the rushes and the flowers? Are the rushes moldy? Are the flowers wilting already?"

"Nothing like that," Liam said, following her down the corridor. "They look fine, and you don't notice that they aren't at first. It's just that they seem to be infested."

"With what? Aphids?" asked Annie.

"Nothing so ordinary," Liam said.

Annie began to hurry. This day was going from bad to worse and she dreaded finding out what was next. She was hurrying down the spiral staircase closest to Eleanor's room when she passed an arrow slit and glanced outside. Lightning flashed near the north tower, a jagged streak of brilliant blue that left a matching streak behind her eyelids when she blinked. She stumbled and nearly fell, but Liam reached out and caught her. After that, she ran down the stairs without looking outside again.

The voices near the great hall were so loud that Annie heard them long before she and Liam reached it. They had to push past the people standing in the doorway to see what everyone was talking about. Even then, Annie didn't see anything wrong at first. The rushes on the floor were fresh and fragrant. The flowers filling the bowls and vases looked just-picked and smelled wonderful. It wasn't until she bent down to examine the rushes that she saw that they were crawling with ladybugs. The peach-colored roses on the closest table were exquisite, until the petals shivered, revealing one big, fat bumblebee after another.

"Those bugs weren't there when we put down the rushes, Your Highness," a young maid said, her lip quivering. "I swear it!"

"I'm sure you're right," said Annie. "No one blames you at all."

When she heard the sound of laughing, Annie stepped into the great hall to see who was there. It was Squidge running across the floor, kicking at the rushes. The moment he spotted Annie, he dashed down the hall with clouds of ladybugs flying up around him.

"This is great!" said the sprite when he reached Annie. "Your wedding guests will have fun with this."

He kicked at the rushes again. Ladybugs flew everywhere, landing on the hem of Annie's skirt, Liam's boots, and the table pushed up against the wall. The people in the doorway behind them moved back as if ladybugs were dangerous.

"Don't be foolish," Annie scolded them. "Ladybugs can't hurt you."

"Maybe they're afraid of the bees," said Liam, eyeing a bumblebee hovering a foot from his face. A few seconds later, the bee flew off, repeating a zigzag pattern.

"We need to talk," Annie said, leading Liam out of the hall and down the corridor, where they couldn't be overheard. "Someone is using magic in ways that makes it obvious that it *is* magic. Whoever is doing this wants me to know that a magic user is behind it."

"You know I don't want to postpone the wedding, but I think we're going to have to," said Liam.

"I know," said Annie. "I'm afraid that if we don't, something even worse is going to happen."

CHAPTER 3

BOOM! AS THUNDER CONTINUOUSLY shook the castle, the dim light coming through the windows flashed blue. A young woman shrieked while a hound hid under a table, its tail between its legs. Annie started toward the door, wanting to see how bad it was outside. Liam went with her and a small crowd gathered behind them as they peered into the darkened courtyard. Rain pounded the ground, sluiced off the roofs of the outbuildings, and gushed from the mouths of stone gargoyles crouching on the tops of the castle walls.

"It looks as if giants are dumping buckets of water on the castle," Liam said, gazing at the deluge. "It shouldn't last long, though. Rain like this never does."

They stood there for a while, willing the rain to let up, but it continued to come down just as hard. "Is this normal?" Squidge said, pushing between Annie and Liam. "It doesn't rain like this in the Moonflower Glade. It would wash away the moonflowers if it did."

"No," Annie said glumly. "It isn't normal here, either."

Voices shouted in the corridor and they turned to look behind them. "I'll find out what's going on!" Squidge declared, and slipped into the crowd. Although Annie could no longer see him, she could tell where he was by the wave of annoyed looks on faces as the sprite bumped into legs and shoved past them.

People made way for Annie and Liam as the commotion in the corridor grew louder. Guards began running up the stairs. Annie and Liam followed on their heels, going all the way to the floor just below the attic. The guards spread out from there, but Annie slipped and slid when she tried to follow Liam down the corridor. She glanced down and found that the floor was wet and water was puddling in the dips and grooves.

"The roof in the south tower collapsed. Most of the other roofs are leaking," a guard told Liam.

"We need buckets and tubs," said Annie. "Something to catch all this water."

She peeked into an open doorway where maids were moving things out from under the dripping ceiling. In the corridor, voices shouted and others swore. Annie turned to see Squidge come running past, chortling as he chased something small and gray. He

23

lunged, then turned suddenly and began to chase it back the other way.

"Is he chasing a squirrel?" Liam asked, frowning after the running sprite.

A woman carrying a bundle of clothes tripped when the sprite ran under her feet. She squealed when she landed in dirty water, drenching herself and the clothes she was carrying. Horace, the old guard, helped her up, then came to Annie when she called to him.

"Tell everyone to take what they can carry downstairs and move what they can out from under the leaks," Annie told him. She turned to Liam, saying, "We should go see how bad it is in the attics."

"That's where we really should put the buckets and tubs," Liam told her as they headed back to the stairs.

They had just started up the last steps, leading a group of guards, when nearly a dozen bats swooped down, some missing them by a hairsbreadth. A squirrel ran past Annie, its tail brushing her foot.

"Blast!" said Liam when he reached the top.

Annie stopped looking out for squirrels and bats and glanced up. She was appalled by what she saw. Although there were no gaping holes as she'd feared, the roof seemed to be leaking everywhere. Water streamed from the ceiling, soaking the odds and ends stored in the attic. The rain beat a continuous rhythm on the roof, still as strong as ever.

A squirrel chattered at her when Annie approached a bench that was leaning precariously on broken legs. Another squirrel popped out from under the bench, and they ran off together, disappearing down the stairs. Bats fluttered overhead, avoiding the leaking water, until they too headed for the staircase.

"I've been in this attic countless times when we were looking for spinning wheels, and I never saw any squirrels or bats," Annie told Liam. "Where do you suppose they came from? Never mind. I think I know the answer. Magic probably brought them here, just like it ruined my dress."

"I think the rain is a bigger problem than anything else right now," said Liam. "We're going to need a lot of tubs. No one can fix the roofs until after the rain stops."

"I'm sure there are tubs in the buttery that we can use," said Annie. "And there may be more in the cellars. I seem to recall seeing some there when I searched the castle. Horace, if you come with me, I can show you where I saw them."

"If you're going to the cellars, I think I should go with you," Liam said, glancing toward the stairs. "I want to see how they're faring. This much water has to go someplace."

As they approached the main level again, Annie heard her father giving orders to his men. She heard her uncle King Daneel's voice as well. They were gone when she got there, so she continued on to the cellars located under the kitchen and the buttery. When she opened the door, she remembered how narrow and dark the stairwell was, and paused at the top of the stairs.

"I'll fetch a torch, Your Highness," said Horace, bustling off down the corridor.

"Do you hear something?" Annie asked Liam as they peered down the stairs.

"It sounds like a squeaky hinge," he replied. "What do you suppose it is?"

A shape moved in the shadows and a large rat appeared on the top step, squinting at the light and twitching its pointy nose. Annie hopped back as two more rats joined it. All three rats darted out of the doorway and down the corridor. A moment later, a small flood of rats poured from the cellar, heading toward the kitchen.

"Cook isn't going to like that," said Annie.

Liam laughed. "I've seen her cat. That thing is mean enough to handle twice as many rats! But if there are rats down there, are you sure you want to go into the cellars?" he asked Annie. "Horace and I can go without you."

"I'm going, too," Annie told him, although she crinkled her nose and held the hem of her gown above her ankles when Horace arrived with a torch and they finally started down the stairs.

Annie was as pleased that they didn't see any more rats in the cellar as she was to find tubs stored beside the baskets of root vegetables. She was still hoping to find a few more tubs when they came across a partly flooded area in the back. The water was already spilling over into the adjoining rooms, and Annie gasped when she saw something in the water move.

"Water snakes," said Liam, herding Annie toward the door. "The river lies just beyond that wall. It must have risen enough to breach its containment. If this rain continues much longer, we'll be in real trouble. I'll send men down here to get these tubs and salvage what food they can before the water gets much higher. Horace, are there any prisoners in the dungeon?"

The old man nodded. "Two. A chicken thief named Billium and Ned Brady, a man that married three women in three different towns."

"The jailer is going to have to find someplace else to put them," Liam said. "If this cellar is flooded, the dungeons are at risk as well. Here, Horace, we can each take a tub now. Annie, could you carry the torch?"

They had started up the steps with Annie leading the way when the stairwell shook. "The floor doesn't shake like that unless both drawbridges are raised at once," said Annie. "I wonder what's happening now."

"You mean what *else* is happening," Liam muttered.

Annie had to stop at the top of the stairs to let a group of soldiers run past. "What's going on?" she asked the last soldier.

The man slowed enough to say, "There's an army advancing on the castle. It was raining so hard we didn't see them until they were halfway to the drawbridge."

"Do you think it's a real army?" Annie asked Liam as he set the tub on the floor. "Someone has been using a lot of magic here today. The army might be an illusion. If the rain lets up, I might be able to hear the magic if it's there."

"Then I think we should have a look," said Liam. "Horace, get some men to help you take care of these tubs and see that the food and the rest of the tubs are brought up. The princess and I are going up on the battlements to see this army."

❧

The rain was pouring as hard as ever when they reached the courtyard. Despite the oiled cloth capes they wore, they were soon drenched from the waist down. As the gusts grew stronger, the capes flapped wildly so that Annie and Liam had to fight to hold on to them. Soon the water was trickling through the seams, making them both shiver.

Annie stepped gingerly across the courtyard, try-ing not to slip on the slick stones as she made her way around the growing puddles. The first frog surprised her, but by the time she and Liam reached the far wall and the steps leading up to the battlements, the frogs seemed to be everywhere.

Fortunately, there weren't any frogs on the steps. Because the stairs were too narrow for people to walk side by side, Liam climbed behind Annie to catch her if she slipped. The well-worn stones were so slick that climbing demanded all her attention. It seemed to take forever to get to the top, but when she did she saw that Squidge was already there, his little arms clinging to the wall as he craned his neck to see over the edge. Finding a place to stand behind one of the crenellations, she glanced at the sprite. "Careful," she said. "This wind is strong enough to blow you away."

"Pfft!" Squidge replied. "Not me!"

Annie wasn't so sure that the wind wasn't going to blow *her* away, so when Liam joined her, she moved closer until their sides touched, giving her some small sense of security. She glanced down at the moat, which was overflowing its banks, then to the far right, where the Crystal River was higher and more turbulent than she had ever seen it. When Liam moved beside her, her gaze followed his arm as he pointed over the wall to the middle of the field that lay beyond the moat.

"Who are they?" she asked, squinting at the blurry shapes half-hidden in the pouring rain.

29

"I can't tell," said Liam. "The wind is whipping their banners around and I can't make out their sigil."

"What's a sigil?" Squidge asked.

"It's a king's emblem or sign," said Annie. "They put it on flags so people know who they are."

Liam leaned closer until the hood of his cape brushed hers. "Can you hear any magic?" he asked.

Annie shook her head. "All I can hear is the wind and the rain. From what I can see, the army looks real enough, but that doesn't mean anything."

The wind grew even stronger now, pushing them against the raised part of the wall. Annie was glad the crenellations were there, or she was sure she and Liam would have been blown over the edge. When it occurred to her that Squidge might need help, it was already too late. She had just started to reach for him when the wind plucked him from the wall and tossed him into the air like a cat might toss a mouse.

"Ahhh!" wailed the sprite as he cartwheeled over the moat and above the advancing army, finally disappearing over the forest.

"Squidge!" Annie cried, reaching for him with one hand while the other gripped Liam's.

"He's gone!" Liam said in disbelief. "I should have held on to him."

"Or I should have," said Annie. "I can't believe that just happened! The poor little guy!"

The wind was already dropping. Within moments it was little more than a light breeze.

"Let's get down off this wall before the wind starts up again," Liam said, putting his arm around Annie.

"Or some other awful thing happens," she said, dreading the climb back down.

CHAPTER 4

ANNIE AND LIAM were about to start down the stairs when the blast of a trumpet made them run back to the wall. A trumpeter dressed in soggy blue-and-red clothes stood dripping by the foot of the draw-bridge. Beside him, a herald dressed in the same colors clutched a scrolled parchment to his chest. When the trumpeter had finished playing, the herald held up the scroll, but it was so wet that it tore in half when he tried to unroll it.

"I bet the ink has run, too," Annie whispered to Liam. From the disgusted look the man gave the parch-ment, she was sure that she was right.

"Hear ye, hear ye!" the herald said, squinting at the pieces of parchment. After a moment, he gave up, dropping his hands and the parchment with them. "King Dormander of Scorios gives you one chance to surrender your castle before he will take it by force," the herald shouted, then ruined his dramatic announcement by sneezing. Turning on his heel, the man stomped away, splashing through a puddle while the trumpeter hurried to catch up.

"Who is King Dormander?" Annie wondered out loud.

"I've never heard of Scorios, either," said Liam. "Did you see the sigil? It looked like some sort of fish chasing a dragon."

Annie shrugged. "That's new, too. I don't think they're from around here. But that doesn't make any sense. Why would a stranger demand that we give up our castle?"

"Let's go see what your father has to say," Liam said, heading for the stairs.

"I'll join you in a little while," Annie told him. "There's too much magic here today. I need to find out who's responsible."

❧

Annie's chamber was dark when she walked in, just as it was on every rainy day. She didn't bother lighting a candle, however, but walked straight to the far corner, where the magic mirror leaned against the wall. She stood contemplating the swirling mist in the mirror for a moment before finally saying, "All right, mirror, I'm not in the mood for games. Tell me what's going on today."

The face slowly formed in the mirror. As it came into focus, Annie thought it looked annoyed. "You know you have to ask a question if you want an answer."

"Fine," Annie snapped. "Who is responsible for the magic that ruined my wedding?"

"Now *that* I can answer!" said the mirror.

A procession of faces seemed to float through the frame, one after the other. Annie recognized some of them; others she had never seen before. Of the ones she did know, they all lived in Treecrest and were either fairies or witches.

"All of them?" Annie asked, incredulous.

"I can tell you their names, if you'd like. But I must warn you, your sister used up most of my energy with all those questions. I won't be able to show you much more than—"

"Then answer another question instead," Annie interrupted. "Who is this King Dormander?"

The face that appeared in the mirror now was of an older man with graying hair and a curly beard that covered his chin. His eyes were an intense blue that seemed to look directly into Annie's. This time when the mirror spoke, the voice started out faint. "King Dormander is the . . . ," the mirror said, fading away to silence.

"He is the *what*?" Annie demanded, taking a step closer to the mirror, but the space inside the frame was empty without even the swirling mist. Annie gave the frame a smart rap with her knuckle. "You can't do this! I have a lot of other questions to ask you! Why are witches and fairies using magic to ruin my wedding? Why is that king here now? What does he really want? Are the witches and fairies on his side? I bet that's it! I bet they were trying to distract us so he could walk right in and take over!"

When the mirror didn't answer, Annie spun around, unaware that her hands were fisted and her jaw was clenched. Her mind raced as she stalked to her father's meeting room, where a passing maid said he was consulting with King Daneel and King Berwick. She found them there, talking to Liam and Beldegard, while the three queens listened.

"I questioned the magic mirror," Annie announced as soon as the door was closed behind her. "It seems that just about every witch and fairy in the kingdom is working against us. Does anyone have any idea why they might be angry with us, or want to help some foreign king?"

"All the witches and fairies?" said her mother. "But we invited them to the wedding! I wondered why none of them had shown up yet. I suppose they were planning this all along."

"Do you really think they're allied with this King Dormander?" asked Beldegard. "The magic started before he showed up."

"I think they were trying to distract us with the rain," said Annie. "Poor Squidge getting carried off by

35

the wind like that. He was just trying to help! I feel awful. We'll have to tell the fairy Moonbeam. He was her helper and he—"

"That's exactly what we should do!" cried Queen Karolina. "We'll find Moonbeam and ask her to help us. Don't you see, with all this magic being used against us, we need a magic user of our own. Moonbeam is the only one I know with a connection to our family."

"A friendly connection, you mean," Annie said. "But she isn't from Treecrest."

King Halbert nodded. "Exactly, so she won't be aligned with the fairies who mean us harm. I think it's an excellent idea, my dear," he said to his wife. "From what I've been told, most of our supplies have been damaged in the rising water, and the wells are in danger of being contaminated. We won't be able to withstand a siege for long, especially if this rain continues. I'll send some of my best men in a few hours. They can leave under cover of dark and go find Moonbeam."

"How will they know where to look?" asked King Daneel. "Moonbeam helps so many people, it's difficult to find her even at the best of times."

"They can start at the Moonflower Glade," said Liam. "That is her home."

Annie shook her head. "Squidge told us that she's off doing something with her new husband."

"It will do for a start," King Halbert announced. "I'll have the men leave as soon as the sun sets."

༜

That night, everyone was busy. While King Halbert, King Daneel, and Captain Sterling, the captain of the guard, discussed siege strategy, Queen Karolina and her sister-in-law, Queen Theodora, consulted with the steward about the supplies needed to withstand the siege. Everyone else took turns eating the food that had been prepared for the wedding and emptying out the buckets being used to collect rainwater. Although Annie, Liam, and their friends had helped before supper, after they ate they returned to help the people on the top floor.

The rain stopped falling a few hours after sunset. Annie was carrying a bucket sloshing with rainwater to pour out of a window when the sudden silence made everyone pause and look up at the ceiling. "Do you think it's stopped for good?" one maid whispered to another.

Everyone seemed to be holding their breath, but when the patter didn't begin on the roof again, some of them dared to smile. As people started moving and chatting, Liam took Annie's chin in his hand and tilted her head so that her eyes met his. "You don't seem happy that the rain finally let up. Why is that?"

"Because I'm afraid it just means that something else is about to happen. It's been that kind of day. It's hard to believe that this is—well, was—still our wedding day," she said, biting her lip when it threatened to quiver.

"I know what you mean," Liam said, and leaned down for a kiss. When she moved her head to look into his eyes, he smiled and pulled her closer. "Our wedding just wasn't meant to happen today. Don't worry, we'll choose another day and everything will be perfect."

"I suppose," Annie said with a shuddery breath.

"Your Highness," a guard said, appearing at her side. "King Halbert would like to see you in his meeting chamber."

Annie nodded. "I'll be right there," she told him, then turned back to Liam. "Let's hope it's good news this time."

"I agree," said Liam. "We're due for a change."

ॐ

Annie knew from her father's expression that it was bad news. The tapestry that hid the secret passage leading from his meeting room had been taken down, revealing the dark opening and allowing the dank, musty air to fill the chamber. The only other people in the room were her mother, Captain Sterling, and the two guards who had been sent to find Moonbeam. Annie thought the guards looked odd, but it wasn't until she drew closer that she knew why. They were drenched from the knees down, having waded through the half-flooded tunnel, but the rest of their clothes were wet with something other than water. A pale green, slightly lumpy liquid coated them from the tops of their heads to their knees, and they both had a very odd smell.

"What happened?" Liam asked the men. "Why are you back so soon?"

"There was a fog," one of the guards drawled, speaking so slowly that he was hard to listen to. "The forest is filled with it."

"You can't see through it," said the other man just as slowly. A drop of something wet and viscous dripped down his forehead. At first, Annie couldn't tell that the man was moving his hand to wipe it away, the movement was so sluggish. Watching him was so irritating that she took out her own handkerchief and wiped his forehead herself. His movements speeded up at her touch.

"What is this stuff?" she asked, keeping her hand on the man's forehead.

"The fog," he replied in a normal voice. "It's as thick as pea soup."

Liam sniffed, then swiped at the man's sleeve with one finger. "It smells like pea soup." He gave it a tentative taste and laughed. "It is pea soup, though it's a bit too salty for my taste. Look, there are even bits of ham."

"More magic," said Annie. "They must have made the rain stop so it wouldn't wash away the fog."

"If you can't see through the fog and it slows you down like this," the king said, gesturing to the two guards, "no one is going to be able to get out to find Moonbeam."

"I can," said Annie as she stepped away from the guard. As soon as she was no longer touching him, his movements slowed again. "It's magic," Annie continued. "Other than being disgusting, the fog shouldn't bother me."

King Halbert shook his head. "I can't allow you to go. We don't know what else they might have lying in wait out there. You'd be vulnerable if you ran into a non-magical threat."

"Which is why I'm going with her," said Liam. "Annie can get me through the fog, and I'll make sure she stays safe."

"You can't go, Annie!" cried the queen. "This isn't like the other trips you've made on our behalf. That's an army out there. Who knows what they'd do if they captured you."

"They won't get the chance," said Annie. "If we can't see through the fog, neither can they. And Liam is the best sword fighter I've ever seen. No one will hurt me with him at my side."

"But—" the queen began.

"The army is camped south of the castle," Annie explained. "They'll be counting on the fog to keep us from venturing out. Liam and I will head north. If there's just the two of us, we should be able to avoid any patrols."

"We can find horses north of here," Liam told her. "If we're on horseback, we should be able to reach the bridge and cross into Floradale before sunrise."

Annie could tell that he found the prospect exciting. He'd been such a good sport about planning the wedding, but she'd known he'd been bored. She was sure that a mission like this would be the kind of thing he'd enjoy.

"How long will it take you to get ready?" asked her father.

The queen sighed. She had to know that if King Halbert was agreeing to it, nothing she could say would change his mind.

"An hour," Annie said, glancing at Liam for confirmation.

He nodded, saying, "We just have to pack a few things."

"Then our thoughts and prayers will go with you," said Queen Karolina. "I suppose that if anyone can find Moonbeam, it's you two."

CHAPTER 5

THEY WERE ON THEIR WAY to change their clothes and gather what they needed when Annie stopped Liam. "I think we should travel in disguise, at least while we're in Treecrest," she said. "For all we know, King Dormander has lookouts all around the kingdom."

"You mean you're going to dress as a boy again?" he asked.

Annie had dressed as a boy while looking for a prince to kiss her sister awake. Not only was it a good disguise, but it allowed her to travel more comfortably without long skirts to weigh her down. Sometimes she wished she could dress like a boy more often.

"Yes, I'm going to dress like a boy, but not the way I usually do. I think we should dress as farm boys so we're not associated with the castle at all. If anyone recognized us for who we really are, word would get out that we had left the castle and people would come looking for us."

"I thought we'd wear black cloaks so no one would see us in the dark," said Liam.

"And look doubly suspicious in the daylight?"

Liam shrugged. "We can wear disguises if you want to, but do we have to use made-up names, too?"

"Hmm," said Annie. "That's not a bad idea. It wouldn't do to have you call me Annie when I'm supposed to be a boy."

"I was joking!"

"Well, I'm not. If we're traveling as farm boys, I should have a boy's name and I should call you something other than Liam."

"All right, *Seth*," Liam said with a smile.

"That will work," said Annie. "Try to find some old clothes, *Ruben*. And the boots should be scuffed and worn."

"In an hour?"

"I'm going to send a maid down to the stable to find a boy my size, wearing the oldest, most worn-out clothes. I'll trade his clothes for some I wore as a disguise before. They're too nice for me to wear now, but one of the stable boys would probably like them. The maid might have to look harder for someone with boots that will fit me. You can do the same if you want."

"I will," said Liam. "But does my name have to be Ruben? I always thought of myself more as a Dirk, or Cliff . . ."

Annie laughed. "I'll see you in one hour," she said, and gave him a quick kiss before hurrying off.

෭

Only her father and Captain Sterling were there when Annie returned an hour later. The tapestry that covered the secret passageway was back in place, and she glanced at it with a questioning look when she sat at the table.

Her father must have noticed, because he glanced at the tapestry as well, saying, "That passage leads south, and you're headed north. There are other secret passages, you know. This is just the one our family has used most often. There are two more; one comes out by the river, but it's flooded now."

When he looked toward Captain Sterling, the man nodded and said, "You'd have to be a fish to use it today."

"The other passage has stood up to all this rain fairly well and you should be able to use it," said the king. "The captain sent two of his men to check it out. There's some water, but they say it isn't too bad. The tunnel comes out to the east in the middle of a hayfield."

Annie glanced at the door as Liam walked into the room. He wore clothes as stained and dirty as the ones she had on, but while Annie's fit and she was pleased to have them, Liam looked uncomfortable and kept plucking at the neck of the rough-cloth tunic. Standing in the doorway, he gave Annie a rueful smile before saying to the king, "We're ready to go, Your Majesty."

Annie tucked her hair further under her cap as she got to her feet. She shouldered the knapsack holding the things she was taking with her, and stepped back as her father and the captain went to the door. Catching up with Liam, she looked him up and down and said, "Do those clothes fit all right?"

"They're fine," Liam said, rubbing at his neck. "Soft living has spoiled me. This shirt feels like it's covered in grit. I don't know if it's ever been washed."

"It's hard to wash your clothes if you own only one outfit," said Annie. "I'm sure the stable boy is enjoying the clothes you traded for that."

"I'm sure he is," Liam said.

❧

Annie had no idea where the entrance to the passage-way might be located, but she wasn't expecting to go to a little-used bedchamber that was filled with a wedding guest's belongings.

"Your friend Snow White has been using this room," said King Halbert. "Your mother had to invite her to visit in her chamber to get her to leave. There's no need to reveal a secret passage to a guest."

They all watched as Captain Sterling lifted a flickering candle from a sconce on the wall, then turned the sconce once all the way around. There was a grating sound and a puff of dust as a crack as tall as Annie opened in the wall. The captain continued to turn the sconce, opening the crack until it was wide enough to admit a short man. "That's as big as it gets," said the captain. "Here, take this." Lighting a torch with the candle he'd taken from the sconce, he handed the torch to Liam and moved out of the way.

"Be careful, my dear," the king told Annie. "You know, I wouldn't want you to go if there was any other way."

"I know, Father," Annie said. She did something then that she'd never done before, and surprised herself by doing it now. She stood on her tiptoes and kissed her father's cheek. The king looked startled, and more than a little pleased.

Liam was stepping through the crack in the wall when Annie turned to look for him. "The stairs look dry from here," he said, thrusting the torch deeper into the opening.

Annie followed him, trying to stay in the light of the torch. The stairs were steep, each step barely as long as her foot, with the walls of the stairwell only inches from her shoulders. She climbed down slowly, her hands brushing the wall to keep her balance. Small spaces didn't usually bother her, but once she heard the crack in the wall close behind her, she had to fight a moment of panic. The only things that prevented her from freezing where she stood were Liam's presence and the thought that she'd be left in the dark if she didn't keep going.

"The torchlight is reflecting off water ahead," said Liam. "I can't tell how deep it is, but it definitely covers the floor. Careful, this step is underwater. And . . . oh, good. We've reached the bottom."

Annie took the last few steps even slower than before. Her boots were well worn and the leather cracked; water filtered through as soon as she touched the bottom step. When the floor leveled out before her, she was relieved that the water came up only as high as her ankles. Although the boots soon filled with water and felt heavy and clumsy, they cushioned her feet better than the dainty slippers she normally wore.

"Watch out," Liam told her. "The floor is uneven here."

Annie paused, and in that moment heard the faint hum of magic. It was a steady pulse, as if the earth surrounding them had a heartbeat. She thought that it was probably the sound of some magic used long before to reinforce the sides of the tunnel. "We need to go faster," Annie called to Liam. "I think this tunnel is in such good shape only because someone used magic to make it stronger. The longer I'm in here—"

"The weaker the magic," Liam finished. "I understand. Just be careful, there are some sticks floating up ahead and . . . Blast! They aren't sticks, they're water snakes. Whatever you do, don't trip and fall. And don't stop."

"In other words, step carefully, but be quick about it!" grumbled Annie. "Great! As if we don't have enough to worry about already." Annie was frightened, and talking seemed to help. It blocked out the sound of the changing magic, the beat growing fainter around her. It also took her mind off the snakes. She had never liked snakes, but facing them in the dark when she couldn't really see them was truly terrifying.

There was a splash in front of her and Liam yelped. The light of the torch dipped and swayed, then grew steady again a moment later. "Are you all right?" Annie called to him.

"The ground is really uneven here," Liam said. "I tripped, but I caught myself against the wall. Get away from me, snake!" The light wavered again as Liam kicked out and something hit the side of the tunnel. "Hurry, Annie, the water is rising and bringing more snakes with it!"

"How long is this tunnel?" Annie cried as she hurried to catch up with Liam. She still had her hands on the walls on either side, which were dripping water now.

"I think we must be under the moat. We should be past it soon, then under dry land for at least a few hundred feet more."

Something snagged Annie's boot, tugging so that she almost lost her balance. She braced her hands against the wall and shook her foot, but whatever was there seemed to be stuck. Lifting her boot, she shook it as hard as she could. The *thing* slapped the wall with a sickening, wet sound, but its weight was still there when she set her foot down again. Not wanting to know what it was, she kept going, dragging the weight with her. A stream of water broke through the wall seconds after she had passed by, spraying her back. Although she'd thought she was moving as quickly as she could, she went even faster now.

"The floor is slanting up," Liam called to her. "I think the water level is dropping. Yes, it's definitely lower. How are you doing?"

"Fine," Annie said through gritted teeth. The *thing* was still stuck to her boot, and she was dragging it forward with every step. If it was a snake, as she feared, she wasn't going to do anything about it until she could see what she was doing. She was sure that Liam would help her if she told him, but it would mean they would have to stop. Although the tunnel was dryer now, it could still collapse around their ears. The thing on her boot would just have to wait.

As they trudged through the tunnel, Annie could tell that it was definitely angling upward. Her boots felt like lead weights and she could hear the thing dragging behind her each time she moved her right foot.

When Liam stopped suddenly and called, "We've reached the end of the tunnel," Annie wasn't sure what he meant at first. If they'd reached the end, why had he stopped?

"There's something blocking the way," Liam called to her. "I just . . . Ah, I see. We turn here and . . . Come on, Annie. You have to walk around the boulder and you'll be outside."

The light from the torch vanished along with Liam, but an instant later it was back as he shoved the torch into the tunnel. Annie hurried then, shuffle, drag, shuffle, drag, to the end of the tunnel, which was indeed blocked, spying the opening to her left only when she was feet from the boulder.

Annie sighed with relief as she stepped out into the cool night air. They were in a field with a mound of boulders behind them. Hay grew thigh high on every side, but they couldn't see more than a few feet because of the thick green fog that surrounded them.

"I think I should put out the torch," Liam told her, his voice slowing with each word. "The light might make the fog around us brighter and give us away."

"Not yet," Annie said, pointing at her foot. "There's something on my boot and I'll run a lot faster without it. I need your light to see what it is."

"Annie," Liam said as he lowered the torch. "You've been walking with *that* on your foot?"

A snake as long as her arm lay stretched out on the ground behind her. Its body was limp and battered, and its fangs were stuck in her boot.

"I tried to shake it free," Annie told Liam. "But its fangs are really in there."

"First of all, let's make sure it's truly dead," Liam drawled. Even though the fog clinging to his skin and clothes slowed his movements, it took him only a moment to find a fist-size rock. When he was sure the snake couldn't possibly be alive, he grabbed its head and unhooked its fangs from her boot. "I'm glad you suggested we wear these heavy boots. If you'd worn anything else, the snake would have bitten you."

"I know," Annie said, not wanting to think about it. "Which way should we go?"

"Your father said the tunnel led east. In that case, the forest should be straight ahead."

"Don't put the torch out yet," Annie said as she peered into the fog. "It's so thick, I don't think anyone could see the light." She took a step forward and the fog retreated so that she stayed in a clear circle about eight feet wide wherever she went. "Look, the fog is moving away from me. I think I . . . Liam?" He had been there a moment before, but the fog had already swallowed him.

"I'm right here, Annie," he said, his voice faint although she knew he couldn't be far.

"Don't move. I'm coming to find you," she said, retracing her steps. He was there, right where she had left him. "And my name is Seth, remember?"

"Uh, right. Sorry, Seth," Liam said with a grin.

Annie noticed that while he was covered with the sticky fog, none of it had touched her. "Hold my hand and don't let go," she told him. "We need to get to the forest."

"The fog will probably be there, too," said Liam, his words normal now that he was in contact with Annie.

"I know, but at least we'll be able to hide there when the fog disappears."

Walking hand in hand, they began moving toward the forest. Although Annie doubted anyone could see the light, she still felt better when they finally reached the trees. She was familiar with the woods around the castle, having explored them as a child and again with Liam when they needed to get away from everyone. Shortly after entering the forest, she figured out where they were and led the way to the road. The fog was so thick that they could walk beside the road without being seen by riders.

When they finally stopped to rest beside a stream, Liam handed Annie the torch and stepped into the water, staying within the fog-free circle that surrounded her. "I'm going to rinse this gunk off," he said. "I can't stand the smell much longer. And I hate that you have to hold my hand so I can walk and talk normally. I'd rather hold your hand because I want to, not because I have to. Would you mind sitting right there so I can see what's around me?" He pointed at a rock by the edge of the water.

Annie sat down and leaned over to inspect her boot. One of the fangs had broken off in the leather when Liam had pulled the snake free. Shuddering, she looked away, and her eye caught movement in the fog. Holding the torch higher, she tried to see it again, but it was no longer there. All she was left with was the impression of two bright green circles looking out at her from the swirling, drifting fog.

"Uh, Ruben, are you almost ready to go?" she asked.

"Just a minute," Liam said, dunking his head in the water to scrub the foggy goo out of his hair. When he stood again, he shook his head, sending droplets flying everywhere. Some reached Annie, but the two green circles were back and she was watching them draw closer. She thought they were eyes, but had no idea what kind of creature had eyes like those.

Liam climbed out of the stream and took Annie's hand again. "I think we have company," she whispered.

Turning to see what she was looking at, he frowned and bent down. "I can take care of that," he said, picking up a rock.

The eyes seemed to be watching him as he pulled back his arm and threw the rock between them. Suddenly, the eyes separated, moving farther apart. Annie gasped. Maybe they weren't eyes after all. When the green circles didn't leave, Liam picked up another rock and chucked it directly at the circle on the right. It disappeared as if a light had gone out. As Liam took aim again, the second circle darted out of sight.

"What do you think they were?" asked Annie.

"Heck if I know," said Liam. "But I didn't like the way they were watching us."

They started walking again then, although Annie kept looking back to see if the green circles had returned. "You mentioned getting horses," she said after a while. "How are we going to do that? We're past Shelterhome and we don't dare go there anyway. There are bound to be enemy soldiers in the town. But I don't know of any stables in this direction."

"I wasn't planning to visit a stable," Liam said, scratching his neck. "There are plenty of farms around and I'm sure some of them have horses."

"I do recall seeing horses in a field a few miles from here," said Annie.

"Then lead the way," Liam replied.

They were more than halfway through the forest when the fog began to dissipate. The torch gave out an hour or so later, leaving them to stumble through the pre-dawn gloom. By the time they reached the edge of the forest, the sky was growing lighter in the east and they could see a farmer's fields. Only a few thin green tendrils of fog floated between the trees.

"The sun is coming up," Annie pointed out. "There will be people on the roads soon."

"I'm trying to decide which horses to go after. I think the bay for me and the chestnut for you."

Annie gave the horses an appraising look. "I think they're probably cart horses. I don't know if we can ride either of them. Besides, isn't it up to the farmer which horses he'll sell to us? Not all horses are for sale."

"They are at the right price," Liam said, eyeing the fence that separated them from the field. "If I was planning to pay for them."

Annie was shocked. "You're going to steal these horses!"

"Well, I'm not going to go to the farmer's cottage to introduce myself. It's better if the farmer doesn't see us at all. Then he won't have anything to tell Dormander's spies if they ask. Don't worry, I'll bring the horses back and pay the farmer for their use after Treecrest returns to normal."

"In the meantime, he won't have a horse to pull his wagon!"

"In the meantime, we'll be risking our lives to make sure he has a good king on the throne to keep him safe! And if it means we steal a horse, then so be it!"

"You have a point," Annie said. "I just don't think it's right to steal."

"I don't think any of this is right," said Liam as he took two lengths of rope from his knapsack. "But we don't have a choice. Now, do you want to help me catch these horses, or do I have to do it myself, *Seth*?"

"I'm coming, *Ruben*. Why don't we see who can catch their horse first?"

"That doesn't seem like a fair challenge," said Liam. "I'm very good with horses."

"It isn't a fair challenge," Annie admitted. "Maybe I should give you a head start."

"Ha!" said Liam. Dropping one of the ropes at Annie's feet, he ran to the fence and vaulted over with the other rope clutched in his fist.

Before Annie followed Liam over the fence, she took the time to knot the rope into a makeshift halter, then stopped to pull up some long, sweet grass. Liam was hurrying toward the grazing bay as Annie climbed the fence and walked into the field. Making soft, encouraging sounds, she moved toward the chestnut horse, holding the grass in front of her. When she glanced at Liam, he was following the bay around the field. Each time he was within a few feet of the horse, it walked off.

Annie grinned. So much for his head start. She had learned how to ride from the stable boys when she was a little girl and had often gone into the field with them to bring in horses. She'd learned long ago that chasing a horse down was not the best way to catch one. Annie glanced at the chestnut again. It was a big, sturdy gelding, with a homely head and a kind eye. She already knew that she liked him.

When the chestnut finally came close enough, Annie gave him the grass, then began stroking his neck, finding an itchy spot up under his mane. The horse's eyes were half-closed with contentment when Annie slipped the halter on.

Hoping that the farmer had ridden the horse as well as made him pull a cart, Annie led the gelding to a large rock, using it as a mounting block to climb on. The horse turned his head to glance at Annie, but didn't seem to mind. When Annie looked for Liam, she saw that he was still following the bay around the field. He seemed irritated when she walked the chestnut to his side.

"Have you come to gloat?" he asked.

"I came to offer you a ride. It's daylight now and I'm surprised the farmer hasn't seen us yet."

"I suppose we could ride together," Liam said, eyeing the gelding.

"I think he could handle that just fine," Annie said, reaching out to give Liam a hand up. "I have no idea what his name is, but I'm going to call him Otis."

"You and your names," muttered Liam as he made himself comfortable behind Annie.

CHAPTER 6

LIAM STARTED GRUMBLING about the horse when they'd ridden less than a mile. "He doesn't have a very comfortable gait," he said. "The other horse would have been better."

"Would you rather sit in front of me?" asked Annie.

"Maybe we'll switch places when we take a break. I remember this place. We rode past that cottage when we were taking Granny Bentbone to the tower."

Annie nodded. "This ride may be uncomfortable, but it's better than traveling in the carriage with that nasty witch."

"It's better because I can hold you close," Liam said, tightening his hold around her as he kissed the top of her head.

"Which is very nice for Annie, but weird if I'm supposed to be your brother, remember?"

"Oops, right," Liam muttered. She could feel his arms relax as he leaned back on the horse, and she couldn't help but smile.

They rode past one small farm after another before the fields gave way to groves of linder trees. As the day grew warmer, Annie began to yawn and her eyelids started to droop. They had been awake since early the day before, and the lack of sleep was finally catching up with her. After a while she dozed, waking suddenly when she swayed and Liam caught her.

"Are you all right?" he asked.

"Just really tired." Annie turned her head to glance at Liam and caught him yawning. "Maybe we should stop and rest for a bit."

"I'm fine," said Liam. "We need to keep going. You can take a nap if you want."

"If you're sure . . . ," Annie murmured, and was asleep before Otis had gone much farther.

Less than an hour later, Annie woke to find herself leaning perilously to the side on a horse that was standing at the edge of the road, nibbling the leaves off a linder tree. "Hey!" she cried, startled, and realized that Liam was leaning, too. His arms were still around her, but now he was about to fall off and take her with him.

"Wake up!" Annie shouted, jabbing Liam with her elbow.

"Huh! What?" he said, and nearly knocked them both off when he struggled to sit upright again.

"That does it," Annie said, swinging down from Otis's back. "We're not going any farther until we've rested."

Liam yawned again as he slid down, landing beside Annie. "We're doing this for you," he said, taking the end of Annie's rope. "I could keep going all day."

"I'm sure you could," Annie said, peering among the trees. "We need to get away from the road. Back in there looks good enough."

It took them a few minutes to get out of sight because Otis kept stopping to strip the leaves off twigs. When they finally reached a spot where they couldn't see the road and doubted that anyone riding by could see them, they tied Otis to a sturdy branch with enough rope that he could nibble the tall grass. Annie lay down in the shade, while Liam sat with his back propped against a tree trunk a few feet away. "I'll keep watch while you rest," he said.

Annie was too tired to argue. She doubted he'd be able to stay awake. Then she was asleep and no longer cared.

❧

The sun was directly overhead when Annie woke. She could hear Otis cropping the grass that grew between the trees, and Liam was still leaning against the trunk. She wasn't surprised to see that he was sound asleep. However, she did think there was something odd about the tree. Its branches looked different and . . .

The high, thin voices of tiny fairies brought Annie fully awake. She closed her eyes until they were no more than slits, and lay there without moving. Peering between her nearly closed lids, she saw that in the short time that she had been asleep, the branches had grown down, creating what looked like a birdcage around her and Liam. Four tiny fairies were perched on the top of the cage, talking.

"I tell you, it's them," said a fairy in a mossy cap. When the fairy turned her head, Annie could see that she was odd looking, with a long nose and the feet of a duck. "You saw how Daisy's sleep-long spell bounced off her." The fairies glanced down at another fairy, curled up at the base of the cage, snoring softly. "The princess is the only one we know who can resist our magic."

"At least we can cast spells on things around her. We hadn't thought of that!" added a male fairy wearing a bluebell cap. At first Annie thought the fairy might have the same rash as the royal ladies at home, but his spots were multicolored and didn't move.

Suddenly Annie recognized the fairies. They had all tried to cast spells on her once. The spells had backfired, doing to them what they had planned to do to her.

The fairy dressed all in bark kicked her foot against the cage. "That can't be the princess. It's a boy. Look at his clothes!"

"It's a girl wearing boy's clothes," said the fairy with duck feet. "Don't you recognize the princess's face? And this other one is definitely the prince. I never got a good look at him before, but he fits the description like a seed in a thistle."

"Are we ready?" said the fourth fairy. She was the prettiest of them all, with softly curling hair and large, dark eyes. Her dress was made of fern leaves; Annie remembered that she was named Fern. "She said to call her as soon as we had the cage made. She's going to be mad that it took us this long."

"It would have been faster if her spy eyes had worked better," said the fairy in the bluebell cap. "A couple of little rocks and they disappeared for good. If it had been me, I would have thrown the rocks right back at him!"

"Enough chatter!" said the fairy with the moss cap. "Voracia! We're ready for you!"

Annie tried not to react when she heard the fairy's name. It was the same fairy who had cursed her sister, Gwendolyn, at her christening. Annie had dealt with the evil fairy only once when she was trying to find a way to break the spell without waiting one hundred years. She hadn't liked her then and had hoped she'd never see her again.

When Voracia didn't appear right away, the tiny fairies became impatient. "What's keeping her? She was the one who said we had to hurry," said the bark-clad fairy. "If she doesn't come soon, I'm going to try out some of my spells on them. I've thought of a few good ones. We can turn the grass into prickers and fill them full of fleas!"

"You know, we can still cast spells on the prince," said the boy fairy. "I have a few I'd like to try."

Annie held her breath. Moving as quietly as she could, she pushed her hand through the tall grass until the tips of her fingers touched Liam's side. She couldn't believe that the fairies thought she was still asleep after they had talked for so long, but she'd take advantage of it as long as she could.

Annie kept her fingers pressed against Liam as the fairy flew between the bars. Aiming his wand at Liam, he made a flicking gesture and silver sparks shot out of the tip. Because Annie was touching Liam, the sparks bounced off him and shot back at the fairy, hitting with enough force to shove him backward. The fairy shook his head as hair began to sprout all over his face and hands. "Noooo!" wailed the fairy, putting his hands to his cheeks.

Liam stirred, the spell broken through Annie's touch. "What was that?" he murmured, sitting up and rubbing his forehead. When he saw Annie looking at him, he gave her a halfhearted grin and said in a groggy voice, "Uh . . . I wasn't asleep. Just resting my eyes."

"How did that happen?" cried the fairy, who was now covered with hair the same colors as his spots. "It was supposed to be him, not me!"

"What's going on here?" demanded a harsh voice. "All you were supposed to do was trap them until I showed up. Serves you right, Hairy Fairy! Ha! That's what I'm going to call you from now on!"

The little fairy ducked his head and flew to his friends while hiding his face in his hands.

Annie sat up, certain that there was no use in pretending to be asleep any longer. She turned to face Voracia. The evil fairy was dressed in black with a tattered red, black, and yellow snakeskin wound through her silver hair. A large black spider brooch was pinned to her chest; Annie blinked when it waved one of its legs at her.

"Mrowr!" wailed a scrawny gray cat shut in a cage that was much too small for it. When Voracia kicked the cage, the cat flattened its ears and crouched as low as it could go.

"So we meet again," Voracia said, displaying the gaps in her teeth when she smiled at Annie. "First of all, I want to thank you for giving me a good reason to arrange this meeting. Not that I needed a reason, but my peers will understand better and not persecute me for giving you what you deserve. I must say, I've been looking forward to this. It's because of you that my two helpers ran off. Pinch 'Em and Poke 'Em were the best helpers I ever had, even if they were lazy, good-for-nothing . . . Ah, well. No time to reminisce. You came to see me and they took advantage of your little visit and ran off, leaving me in the lurch. Now I have to make do with occasional help like these flea brains. Speaking of flea brains, I brought you a small gift."

Bending down, she opened the door to the cage and hauled the cat out by the scruff of its neck. The cat screeched and tried to claw her, but she shook it until its teeth rattled, then shoved it between the bars of the cage holding Annie and Liam.

"Doesn't look like much, does it? I'll take care of that." With a few muttered words and a wave of her hand, the fairy cast a spell on the cat. It began to grow; although it stayed the same shape and color, it wasn't long before the ordinary cat was as big as a small horse.

The cat was not happy. It thrashed its tail and cried, but what would have been a cat-size *Mrowr!* was now a roar that shook the cage so that the tiny fairies fell off. Liam backed away when the cat looked at him, but then it stalked to the wall of the cage and pressed its face between the bars as if it still might fit through.

The cat became angrier when it realized that it was trapped and began to circle the perimeter of the cage, pushing against the bars with its side.

"What are you doing, you stupid animal? Eat them!" screamed Voracia.

When the cat continued to be more interested in getting out than in eating Annie or Liam, Voracia shook her head and told the tiny fairies, "I hardly ever let the thing out to eat. You'd think it would be hungry enough by now! I know. Maybe if they looked more like familiar food. I can't do anything with the girl, but the boy should be easy enough."

She was raising her hand to cast another spell when the little fairies began to protest. "No!" cried Fern. "It won't work!"

"Don't do it!" shouted the fairy wearing the mossy cap.

"Oh, let her," grumbled the fairy in the bluebell cap. "She laughed at me! Call me Hairy Fairy, will you?"

Once again Voracia raised her hand and gestured, only this time she pointed at Liam. Annie grabbed hold of his hand before the evil fairy let the sparks fly. Instead of hitting Liam, the sparks bounced off and flew back at Voracia, just as if she had pointed at Annie. Everyone watched, horrified, as the evil fairy began to shrink, her lank hair became shorter, thick, and brown, and her ears moved to the top of her head and became rounded. When she was as big as a rabbit, a long, thin tail sprouted from her lower back and she fell to the ground, twitching. She continued to shrink and a moment later she was a mouse, just like Annie often saw scurrying across the floor of the castle.

This was a food that the cat could understand. It threw itself against the cage wall, but Voracia's spell that had made it large was already coming undone. In less than a minute it was its normal size again and fit between the bars easily. The Voracia-mouse saw this and took off into the tall grass, although she was not nearly as fast as a real mouse.

"Did you see that!" squealed the fairy wearing the mossy cap. "She turned Voracia into a mouse!"

"Actually, she turned herself into one," Annie said, but the fairies weren't listening to her. They were all looking at her with horror, and when she sighed and got to her feet, they backed away a few feet only to hover as if they weren't sure if they should leave or not.

The sides of the cage had grown closer to Liam than to Annie. By the time she had taken three steps, however, the branches began to droop. As soon as she laid her hand on one, the entire structure fell apart. When Annie looked for the tiny fairies, they had gone.

"Feeling more rested?" Annie asked Liam as he untied Otis's rope from the branch. "Because I don't care how tired we are after this, we're not going to stop again until we cross over the bridge to Floradale."

CHAPTER 7

ANNIE AND LIAM PASSED only a few people on the road, none of whom seemed interested in two boys riding an old chestnut gelding. It was late afternoon by the time they crossed over the bridge into Floradale. The last time they had visited the Moonflower Glade, they had learned of a shortcut when they were leaving. They took it now, traveling south on the main road until they reached a cutoff that led them toward a heavily forested hillside. The sun was setting when they entered the forest. On the other side of the hill, the road turned into a path scarcely wide enough for Otis. After that, it wasn't long before they reached the glade.

Although the trees continued on the left side of the road for as far as Annie could see, they ended abruptly on the right, giving way to pale blue and iridescent white spheres that floated above their heads, tethered to the ground by long, spindly stalks. The moonflowers bumped together, making a gentle tapping sound. Under them lay a soft carpet of a dense grass that felt spongy under Annie's feet when she dismounted from Otis. The unusual plants appeared to fill a large meadow, and because they grew so high off the ground, Annie could easily see under them from one side to the other. She hadn't noticed it when they'd seen the flowers in the daylight, but a pale glow came off them, the glow brightening as night fell.

"I don't think anyone is here," Annie told Liam. "At least, I don't see anyone. Do you?"

"No," he replied, turning to look around. "There's no one here but us. This is incredible. It's pitch-black in the forest, but here it's as bright as if we're in the great hall when all the candles are lit."

"I think they look like full moons on a clear night. They are moonflowers, after all. What do you think about spending the night here? I don't really want to go through the forest now. It seems awfully dark compared to this."

"I was about to say the same thing," said Liam. "I don't think Otis would mind, either."

The horse was nibbling the grass that grew along the edge of the path, moving from patch to patch as if he were starving.

"We should probably tie him to something, but I think he'd break a moonflower stem, and I don't want to tie him in the forest," Annie said.

"I can handle that," Liam told her. Taking the extra rope from his knapsack, he hobbled Otis's two back legs so he couldn't go far if he did wander off. "I don't think he'll want to leave anyway. There's enough grass here to last him for months."

Annie and Liam shared a small supper of bread and cheese. While Annie put away the rest of the food, Liam spread a blanket on the ground. "I've been thinking," he said as he straightened the blanket. "I'm worried about my father. He didn't come to the wedding like he said he would, and King Dormander's army is south of your parents' castle. That was the direction my father would have come from if he'd been on his way."

"You think he might have run into the army? I can't imagine that they would do anything to him," said Annie.

Liam shrugged. "We don't even know why they're in Treecrest or anything about their king. There's no guessing what a complete stranger would do. I just want to make sure my father is all right, that's all."

"Then after we talk to Moonbeam, and we know she's going to go help my family, we'll head straight to Dorinocco to see your father," said Annie.

"Good," Liam replied. "I can live with that. Here, you lie down on the blanket. I don't think the moonflower stalks are strong enough for me to lean against, so I'll prop myself up on our knapsacks."

"I don't think you need to keep watch tonight," said Annie. "This place has its own kind of magic. I can hear a very faint melody, and the tapping of the moonflowers is part of it. People are safe when they're here; I'm sure of it."

"Really?" said Liam. "Because I can sit up and—"

"There's no need," Annie told him. "What you need to do more than anything is get some rest. Tomorrow we have to look for someone who can tell us where to find Moonbeam."

Liam was reluctant to lie down, but when he did, he was the first one to fall asleep. Annie lay on her back, gazing up at the moonflowers, thinking how glad she was to have Liam in her life. She could handle just about anything when he was by her side. As soon as they found Moonbeam, they'd go check on Liam's father, then deal with King Dormander. After that, they could finally get married and . . . Annie fell asleep, listening to the magic of the moonflowers.

It was only a few hours before dawn when Annie woke. The sound had changed, but she couldn't identify what had happened until she looked up and saw that the moonflowers had opened to catch a gently falling rain. Because the edges of the petals overlapped, the flowers caught most of the rain. As far as Annie could tell, very little moisture actually reached the ground. She fell back to sleep a few minutes later, lulled by the rain's patter.

༂

"Where should we ask about Moonbeam first?" Annie asked Liam the next morning. They had already eaten a breakfast of apples, and Otis was ready to go.

"I thought we'd cross over the rainbow bridge and head for Gruntly Village," said Liam.

Annie was surprised. "You want to ask the ogres?"

"They're the only people we know of who live around here," Liam said, shrugging. "If we see anyone else, we'll ask them."

"Then I hope we find someone soon," said Annie. "I know we've met some nice ogres, but most of them are awful. I'd really rather talk to someone else if we can and avoid the ogre village altogether."

"We'll see who we can find," Liam said as he undid the hobbles on the horse's legs. "But first we have to get Otis through the cave behind the waterfall. He's been calm enough up until now. Let's hope he stays that way."

Annie and Liam walked side by side with Liam leading Otis. The horse seemed interested in where they were going, aiming his ears forward and flicking them at every little sound. When they left the Moonflower Glade and entered the forest, he began walking a little faster, as if eager to see what lay ahead. They were among the trees a very short time before the path took them to a sheer rock wall. The path continued on into a cave that led back into the hill. After the first few feet, the cave was cool and dark.

"Hold on a minute," Liam said at the entrance. Digging into his pocket, he took out some crumpled moonflower petals. "I found these on the ground and wanted to see if they still glowed. You carry these and I'll walk with Otis." Handing the petals to Annie, he let her go first and turned to rub the horse's neck.

Annie studied the petals, which were brown and crumbling around the edges. She doubted they would work, so was pleased when she stepped into the dark and the petals began to glow. They weren't as bright as the living petals had been the night before, but their light was enough to help her navigate the turns in the tunnel that led beyond the cave.

At first Otis seemed reluctant to step into the deep shadow, but at a little urging from Liam he shook his head and kept going. With Annie leading the way, they walked around jutting rocks and found their way through the tunnel, coming out behind the waterfall. The roar of the waterfall made Otis nervous, but Liam soothed him enough that they were able to move past the tumbling water and through the underbrush that concealed the tunnel entrance. Everyone was relieved when they came out the other side, especially Otis, who hurried down the path, practically dragging Liam.

The horse didn't stop until they could no longer hear the waterfall. By then the path had taken them to the bank of another stream, slower and gentler than the first. Otis nickered when he saw the water, so Liam led him to the pebbled shore and filled the waterskin while the horse drank. When they were finished,

Annie and Liam climbed on Otis's back and rode the rest of the way to the rainbow bridge.

It was a beautiful bridge, made of alternating bands of ruby, sapphire, amethyst, emerald, and topaz that filled the air above them with color. Normally, Annie would have stopped to admire the bridge, but now she eyed its smooth surface, remembering how it had become slippery when she crossed it the last time, making her fall off into the water. "Do you think we should ride over it or walk Otis across?" she asked Liam.

"We'll ride across," said Liam, urging the horse forward. "And go as fast as we can."

"But what if it becomes slippery while we're on it? Maybe I should get off and let you ride across."

"Stay right where you are!" Liam said as Annie began to wiggle off. "We're doing this together."

Otis had already progressed from a walk to a trot, but Liam wanted him to go faster, so he kicked his heels as hard as he could and the gelding shot across the bridge as if he were a racehorse. He was still galloping when the path angled away from the stream and ran alongside a pasture fence. Liam had just gotten Otis to slow his pace when the bellow of a bull in the pasture beside them startled the horse and sent him galloping again. He almost overshot the path when it turned a corner following the fence line, but Liam had him under control and they sped along the edge of the path, kicking up clods of dirt and mowing down wild daisies and buttercups. When Otis finally slowed to a walk, Liam patted his neck and praised him.

"You know," said Liam, "Otis isn't just a cart horse. I think he was once a gentleman's horse. He has a lot of heart and is very well mannered."

"And he can gallop with the best of them," Annie said, slightly breathless herself. "Look, there are the minotaurs. And there's someone on this side of the fence. Maybe he'll know something about Moonbeam!"

Otis seemed to be too tired to notice the minotaurs, and plodded toward the man with little urging. Liam called out "Hello!" as they approached him.

The man looked up from scratching the nose of an adolescent minotaur and glanced at Annie and Liam. He nodded at them before turning his attention back to the young half man, half bull.

Annie tried to ignore the man's rudeness. "We were hoping to ask you a question."

"I figured there was a reason you stopped," said the man. "Don't get many strangers out this way. What do you want to know? Yes, they are minotaurs. And no, you can't pet them. Big Daddy back there would be happy to gore anyone who touched one of his youngsters, except me, of course."

Annie looked toward the trees where most of the herd was resting. The big male minotaur was watching them and she remembered how agitated he had become the last time they approached his fence.

"Why do you have minotaurs?" Liam asked. "What do you raise them for?"

"People like to have them guard their labyrinths," said the farmer. "You'd be surprised how many people have labyrinths these days."

"We didn't really stop to ask about your minotaurs," said Annie, "although they are very interesting. We were hoping you could tell us how we could find the fairy Moonbeam. She isn't in the Moonflower Glade and we don't know where to look next."

"Now, I don't know the answer to that one. I've never had much to do with Moonbeam. She keeps to her side of Rainbow Creek and I keep to mine. The one you should ask is Footrot. He takes care of the glade when she isn't around. I expect she tells him where she's going and when she's going—if she tells anyone, that is."

"And where could we find this Footrot?" asked Liam.

"If he isn't in the glade, he's probably in Gruntly Village. Spends most of his free time in the tavern."

"Which tavern would that be?" asked Liam. "I seem to recall that there are two, both with birds on the signs."

"Then it would have to be one or t'other, now wouldn't it?" the farmer said, looking at Liam as if he weren't too bright. When the farmer turned back to the young minotaur, Annie and Liam knew that they'd been dismissed.

Within minutes of leaving the farmer, Annie and Liam rode into Gruntly Village. It was much as Annie remembered it, with tall buildings, strange angles, and windows in odd places. There were two taverns—one at either end of the only street. The first tavern had a sign that bore the picture of a duck lying on its back with "X"s over its eyes and the words THE DEAD DUCK underneath. Annie and Liam were about to dismount to go inside when they noticed a small sign nailed to the door. CLOZED FOR REPARES, read the sign in thick black letters. Battered and dirty, it looked as if it had been reused more than once.

"At least we won't have to look for Footrot in both taverns," Annie said as they continued on.

When they saw that the other tavern was open, they slipped off Otis's back and tied him to a post. The horse pinned his ears back and lifted his leg as if to kick the ogre walking toward them. Seeing this, the ogre changed direction and made a wide berth around Otis. Annie glanced up at the sign as they stepped onto the porch. The picture on the Foolish Finch showed a small bird squashed flat by a departing wagon wheel. Somehow, it was even less appealing than the dead duck on the other sign.

The sun was shining when they stepped across the threshold, but inside the tavern, it was cool and dimly lit. As her eyes adjusted to the light, Annie saw that the room was filled with tables, many of them propped up on makeshift legs. A cage holding a single bedraggled finch rested on the table by the door. Deep gouges scarred the floor and walls, although some of them had been filled in and sanded over. As they stepped into the room, Annie saw that the center of the room was empty, the surrounding tables pulled well back. There were at least twenty ogres in the room, crowded around a few tables, and all were so intent on what they were doing that they failed to notice Annie and Liam.

"Let's watch awhile," said Liam, "and see what's going on."

He led the way toward the tables until they were close enough to see. At one of the tables, a group of ogres were drinking from flagons while watching three slugs inch across a slab of wood. Although they were laughing and talking about all sorts of things, their eyes never left the little creatures. Listening to their comments, Annie decided that they had bet on which slug would reach the end first.

At another table, the ogres were comparing two stripes of paint, one red, the other blue. At least Annie thought it was paint, until she realized that they were betting on whether paint would dry faster than blood. She wondered who had contributed the blood sample.

The ogres at the third table were just finishing negotiations when Annie and Liam walked up. Two of the biggest ogres stood and shook hands before stalking to the middle of the room. Another pair of ogres handed them knobby clubs, while the rest jockeyed for seats.

"What are they doing?" Annie asked Liam.

"Bludgeoning contest," said an elderly ogre seated at the table where the slugs were still racing. She recognized him as the ogre who had given her and Gwendolyn directions when they'd visited Gruntly Village before. He had been the only ogre to talk to them in a nice way, chasing off some of the rough young ogres who had been pestering them. When she looked around the room, Annie saw those three ogres there as well, avidly watching the ogres wielding the clubs. She decided right away to stay clear of them.

Annie shuddered when the two ogres in the middle of the room started hitting each other, with the clubs. The resounding thwacks filled the room, but as they continued to fight, the other ogres started talking again, giving the combatants only occasional glances. "How long will those two fight?" Annie asked the elderly ogre.

"Until they get tired of it or one knocks the other out," he replied. "They won't really hurt each other, though. Footrot and Nose-wipe are best friends. They do this at least once a week for fun. Those two love their contests! Look! They're quitting already. Now comes my favorite part—the tooth-spitting contest! My friend Fleemer here is the village champion. But he doesn't compete anymore, do you, Fleemer?"

The old ogre sitting beside him gave Annie a wide-mouthed grin. She could understand why he no longer competed in the tooth-spitting contest. He didn't have a single tooth in his mouth.

"And the winner of the bludgeoning contest is Footrot," announced an ogre with orange hair that stuck up all over his head, "with Nose-wipe coming in a close second."

"How could he not?" Liam whispered to Annie. "There were only two of them."

After laying his club on a nearby table, the bigger of the two ogres clasped his meaty hands together and shook them in the air, as if he'd won something significant. "At least now we know which one is Footrot," Annie whispered back.

Both ogres were grinning when they went to a line painted on the floor at one end of the open space. With their toes on the line, they took turns spitting the teeth they'd had knocked out. Footrot spit two teeth, but Nose-wipe spit three, and all of his went farther.

"And the winner is Nose-wipe!" shouted the ogre with the orange hair.

Footrot clapped his friend on the back, making Nose-wipe stagger. They were walking past Annie and Liam, heading to the back of the room, when Liam said, "Pardon me, Footrot. May I speak to you for a moment?"

"Well, look at you!" bellowed the ogre so that everyone turned to stare. "There's a little human come join us for a day of fun and games." Footrot was over seven feet tall, and he had to look down to see Liam almost as if he were talking to a child. "Impressive win, wasn't it, little man? You want to learn my secret to winning?" The ogre bent down as if he were going to confide something important. "Have an extra-thick skull!" he said, and roared with laughter. Standing up, he winked at his friends and would have walked on if Liam hadn't planted himself directly in his way.

"I need to ask you a question," Liam told him. "It will take only a minute of your time, if you don't mind."

"But I do mind," Footrot said, no longer looking amused. "Why should I waste my time talking to a pipsqueak like you? Out of my way, little man, or I'll step on you."

"Challenge him to a contest," Annie whispered to Liam. "Think of something that you're sure to win."

"Against an ogre?" Liam whispered back.

While the other ogres bet on whether the human would get out of the way or not, Liam looked around the room. His gaze fell on the finch in the cage. Suddenly his expression brightened. "I want to challenge you to a contest," Liam told Footrot. "If I win, you have to answer my question."

"And if I win?" asked the ogre.

"Then you can squash me flat."

Annie gasped. Liam getting squashed had never been part of the plan.

"I can also squash you flat if no one wins," said Footrot.

"Agreed," Liam replied.

"Then you have a deal," Footrot said with a grin. "What is the contest?"

"You have to make the finch sing," said Liam.

Footrot scratched his ear. "They do that? I don't think I've ever heard one sing."

"They sing when they're happy," Liam told him.

"Then bring on the finch!" Footrot ordered his friends. "This fool just told me the secret and I'm going to win!"

The ogres cleared off one of the tables and set the cage in the middle. "Is there anything I can do to help?" Annie asked Liam as Footrot took his seat.

"Stay on the other side of the room," Liam replied. "Don't come near me until it's over."

"Are you sure? Because I can—"

"I'm positive," said Liam. "You'll be helping me a lot if you'll do that."

Annie was confused, but all she said was, "Then I will."

While Annie went to stand by the door, Liam took a seat across from Footrot. "I'll go first!" said the ogre. He stared at the bird for a minute, then crooked one of his fingers to a young ogre and whispered something in his ear. The ogre was laughing when he left the tavern. While he was gone, Footrot poked the finch with one long finger. The finch darted to the other side of the cage.

The young ogre was back in a few minutes. When he approached the table, Footrot held out his hand. The other ogres laughed as the young one dropped a worm onto Footrot's palm. Holding the worm between his thumb and forefinger, Footrot used his other hand to open the door, then draped the worm over the perch. The finch fluttered around its cage until the ogre shut the door again, finally settling down as far from the worm as it could get.

"Eat the blasted worm and be happy!" the ogre said, shaking the cage.

The bird fluttered around madly. Annie was afraid it was going to hurt itself, but then Liam spoke up. "I win by default if you hurt the bird."

"What's that mean?" one ogre whispered to another.

Footrot grunted and set the cage on the table. "That bird doesn't know how to be happy. You'll never get it to sing."

"I can try," said Liam. He waited until the bird settled on its perch again, then did something not even Annie was expecting. Liam began to whistle.

His whistling wasn't very loud, but everyone in the room stopped talking to listen. Annie had heard him sing, which wasn't at all extraordinary, but his whistling was amazing. Liam had told her once that three fairies had given him christening gifts, one of which was the ability to whistle. He had never shown his skill in Annie's presence before, probably because his whistling would be ordinary if she was close by. No wonder he didn't want her near him now!

All eyes were on the finch as Liam whistled the song of a meadow lark greeting the morning sun. He whistled the song of a robin, gossiping with its neighbor. Finally, he whistled the song of a finch, calling to its mate. If Annie had closed her eyes, she would have thought it was the bird singing. And then it was the bird in the cage, answering Liam's call that had been so perfect that even it couldn't tell the difference.

"The winner is the puny stranger!" announced the redheaded ogre.

Footrot waved the other ogres away and nodded to Liam. Annie hurried over to join them, eager to hear the answer to Liam's question.

"What was it you wanted to ask me?" said the ogre.

"I was told that you work for the fairy Moonbeam," Liam began. "She isn't in the Moonflower Glade now. Where can I find her?"

"Is that all? I thought you wanted to know something important! I haven't seen Moonbeam in weeks," said the ogre. "Last time I talked to her, she stopped by to check on the glade, and was leaving again to marry some human. As far as I know, she's up in Loralet with her new husband."

"Can I ask a question, too?" asked Annie. "Do you think the owner of the tavern would sell us the bird in the cage?"

"My mother owns the tavern and I gave her the finch myself," said Footrot. "You might as well take it. The stupid bird doesn't even know when it should be happy."

"Thanks!" Annie said. Snatching the cage off the table, she hurried out the door before the ogre could change his mind.

Liam was right behind her. After helping her up onto Otis's back, he handed her the cage. "Why did you want the finch? The last thing we need right now is to haul around a birdcage."

"I don't want the cage, just the finch," said Annie. "We'll set it free once we're back in the forest. It's obvious that ogres don't know the first thing about taking care of birds."

"I was surprised he gave it to you. I suppose he didn't want it around as a reminder that he lost."

"Or he's nicer than we thought he was," Annie said, remembering the wink Footrot had given her just before she left the tavern.

CHAPTER 8

ANNIE AND LIAM TOOK THE ROAD out of town and soon reached the main road heading north. They stopped when they found a patch of forest so Annie could open the birdcage to release the finch. The little bird seemed too frightened to move at first, so Annie set the cage on the ground and backed away. After a few minutes, the finch hopped out, fluttered its wings, and flew to a nearby tree. Instead of disappearing into the forest, however, it turned to watch Liam help Annie onto Otis's back. It was still there when they rode away.

They traveled for the rest of the day, calling each other Seth and Ruben when anyone else happened to be around. Most of the time, they were alone with no other travelers in sight, and they were able to talk about the things that really mattered to them, like how Annie's family and all the wedding guests were faring back in the castle, and how anxious Liam was to go see his father. They started seeing more people on the road when they drew near to Loralet, but it was evening by then and they knew it was already too late to visit the fairy Moonbeam. When they finally entered the capital of Floradale, they headed straight for the area where the butcher's shop was located, and found an inn with rooms available.

Otis was happy to let a stable boy lead him into a clean stall in the stable behind the inn. When they were sure that the horse was well cared for, Annie and Liam got themselves a room. After a quick supper of venison stew and coarse bread, they climbed the stairs, yawning.

"Why did we get one room?" Annie asked when the door to their room was closed. "If you need more coins, I brought some, too."

"Shh!" said Liam. "Not so loud. These places have thin walls and we don't want anyone to hear us. I got one room because that's what two farm boys would get. I'll sleep on the floor and you can have the bed."

"Don't you think we can stop pretending now? We're far enough from Treecrest and King Dormander that I think we should be safe."

Liam shook his head. "We can't travel as ourselves yet. People always talk when they see royalty, and we don't want word to get back to Treecrest. You saw how many people we passed outside the gates. If any one of them knew who we really are, King Dormander would learn about it very quickly. I don't want anyone to know we're outside the castle until we bring help back with us."

"Fair enough," said Annie. "I really would have liked a hot bath, but I guess that's going to have to wait, too." She yawned again, covering her mouth with her hand. "It's just as well. I probably couldn't stay awake long enough for them to bring up the water."

"I'm too worried about my father to sleep," Liam said as he spread his blanket on the floor, but a few minutes later neither one was awake.

❧

For the first time on their trip, they both slept through the night without waking. Sunlight pouring through the window woke them the next morning and they were up and out the door minutes later. Although it was still early, the public dining room on the first floor was already crowded. When they appeared at the door, however, the innkeeper's wife was able to find them a table. Neither of them usually ate much in the morning, but a serving girl brought them both cold mugs of cider and plates heaped with coddled eggs, rashers of bacon, and crusty bread still hot from the oven. Annie hadn't thought she was hungry until she smelled the food, and she dug in as if she hadn't eaten in days. Liam didn't notice because he was too intent on his own breakfast, and had already started on a second plate before Annie finished her first.

They were sitting back, pleasantly full, when a young woman came into the dining room to look around. The innkeeper's wife went to talk to her, and the young woman left, looking disappointed. A few minutes later another young woman came in and the same thing happened. This happened three more times. When the innkeeper's wife walked past their table, Liam said, "What did those young women want?"

The woman glanced at the door, saying, "They come by every day, along with half a dozen others. They all want to talk to the fairy Moonbeam. Gertrude isn't working here today, so it's up to me to tell them that Moonbeam isn't back yet, and I have no idea when she'll return. They'll all be back tomorrow, mark my word. Ever since everyone learned that the fairy had helped Eleanor and the prince fall in love, all the less fortunate girls have been hoping that Moonbeam would help them find wealthy husbands as well."

"So Moonbeam isn't in town? Do you have any idea where she went?" asked Annie.

The innkeeper's wife laughed. "What would a boy like you want with Moonbeam? Hoping for a rich wife, are you?"

"Actually, we did need her help with something," said Liam.

The woman sighed. "Sorry, I can't help you any more than I can those girls. I only know what Gertrude tells me. If anyone would know, it would be Gertrude."

"Who is Gertrude?" Annie asked.

"The butcher's daughter, of course," said the innkeeper's wife. "When Moonbeam married the butcher, he declared that his three children had to move out or start supporting themselves. The son got married and moved away and the two girls got jobs. Gertrude works at the inn six days a week, but today is her day off. It's a pity about the butcher shop. It's been closed since Moonbeam and Selbert left. Selbert's son, Jamesey, helped in the shop, and now that he's gone and his father is away, there's no one to run it. These days I have to go halfway across town to get good cuts of meat, and they aren't nearly as good as Selbert's. Ah, if you'll excuse me, someone is waving at me like I'm a runaway coach. Some people don't know the meaning of patience."

As the innkeeper's wife hurried off to help someone else, Liam leaned toward Annie. "Looks like another dead end."

Annie shook her head. "I don't think so, at least not yet. The butcher probably lives above his shop. Let's go pay his daughter a visit. Maybe she knows more than she's told this woman."

౭ఞ

The butcher shop was only a few buildings away on the other side of the street. Liam and Annie were on their way there when they saw a woman and her two daughters walking in the opposite direction. Annie recognized them right away, having met them at the ball where Eleanor met the prince. They were Eleanor's stepsisters, Wilhemina and Zelda, following behind their mother, Lenore. Once again they were arguing.

"It's your turn to make supper tonight, Willie! I did it yesterday," Zelda told her sister.

"You did not! I cooked while you read your silly book. Tell her that it's her turn, Mother! I shouldn't have to do it two days in a row."

"Quiet, both of you!" snapped Lenore as she stopped to face her daughters. "We wouldn't be in this mess if you two had been nicer to your stepsister, Eleanor."

"It wasn't us!" sputtered Willie. "You're the one who made her work like a servant."

"Only because you girls are lazy," Lenore replied.

"I've never seen you do any housework, either!" Willie cried. "I don't think you've ever cooked or washed dishes or swept or cleaned out the fireplace or any of the things you make us do."

"Watch your manners, Willie darling, or you'll be out on your ear!" her mother said. "I'm your mother and I deserve better than this! Even Eleanor will understand when I explain it to her."

"So now you call her Eleanor. You were the one who started calling her Cinderella, Mother. You only like her because she's a princess," grumbled Zelda. "You want her to like us so she'll invite us to the castle."

"Is that such a bad thing?" Lenore said. "We deserve to be there more than she does. I blame it on those two princesses who showed up unannounced. If it hadn't been for them, one of you would have married the prince and we'd be living in the castle right now!"

Annie glanced at the little group as Lenore and her daughters walked past. She tried not to react when Lenore stopped to stare at her as if she looked familiar, but couldn't quite place her. When the woman finally shook her head and moved on, Annie let out a shaky breath, not having realized until then that she'd been holding it in.

When they reached the butcher shop, Liam tried the door just in case. "It's locked," he said. "Do you see another entrance for the house?"

"Not in the front," said Annie. "Maybe we have to go through the alley."

She led the way through the narrow space between the shop and the building next door. There was a door near the back, but it too was locked. "This must be it," Annie said, and knocked.

When no one replied, Liam started thumping the wooden door. "I'm going to keep this up until someone answers or my hand gets tired. We didn't come all this way for nothing."

"Maybe no one is home," said Annie.

"Or maybe the butcher's daughter doesn't want to answer the door," he said, knocking louder.

"Go away!" a voice yelled from inside the house.

"We're not going away until you talk to us," Liam yelled back. When no one came to the door, he began pounding on it and shouting, "Open up!"

Suddenly the door flew open, revealing an angry girl a few years older than Liam. She was wielding a wicked-looking knife like a butcher might use and stood blocking the doorway. "What do you want?"

"To talk to Gertrude," said Annie. "You can put the knife away. We aren't going to hurt you."

"What do you want to talk to Gertrude about?" the girl asked.

"We want to ask her about the fairy Moonbeam," Liam told her.

"I knew it!" the girl said, lowering the knife. "When I first heard the knocking, I said to myself, 'Gertrude, it's another one of those girls wanting to know when Moonbeam will be back. You're not answering the door again today.' But then I heard a man's voice and I thought it was someone with bad intentions. A girl can't be too safe these days. I'm here now, though, so I'll tell you what I tell everybody. I don't know when she'll be back."

She started to close the door, but Liam had put his foot in the way. "Can you tell us where we might be able to find her?" he asked.

93

"I don't know and I don't care," Gertrude said, trying to close the door on Liam's foot. "And even if I did, I wouldn't tell you."

"You sound like you don't like her," said Annie.

The girl opened the door all the way and laughed. It was an ugly sound with no trace of humor. "Would you like someone who marries your father without warning and makes him tell you what to do? He'd been grumbling about our living here for years, but it wasn't until she came along that he did anything about it. Jamesey had to marry the girl he'd been courting and move out to start his own shop. He moved all the way to Harper's Village, so we'll hardly ever get to see him. Papa drove him away because of that woman! And do you know what Papa did to Franny and me? We had to get jobs! Taking care of him and the house wasn't enough. Now we both have to earn our own money."

"Really!" said Annie.

Gertrude nodded. "It's so unfair! The four of us were happy here before that fairy came along. Jamesey helped Papa in the shop when he got really busy, and Franny and I took care of things here at home. Papa gave us money when we needed it and no one had to work like this! And then he married that fairy and everything changed."

"I can only imagine!" Annie told her, trying to look sympathetic.

"And to top it off," said Gertrude, "just a few weeks after Jamesey moved out, Papa took that woman to visit *our brother* and left us here without any money or food in the house. If anyone should have gone on a trip, it was Franny and me. Papa was always working and never took us anywhere, and now look! And the way Moonbeam makes him laugh, why, Franny and I think it's disgraceful. Sure, she's fixed up the house with her magic and given us nice clothes and things, but we still wish Father had never met her. If I ever see that princess who made Moonbeam fall in love with my father, I'll give her a piece of my mind!"

"So you're sure you won't tell us where they went?" said Liam, removing his foot from the doorway.

"No, I won't! So don't ask again," Gertrude said, and slammed the door in their faces.

Annie couldn't help but laugh as they walked away. "She doesn't realize it, but she just gave me that talking-to!"

"And told us where to find her father and Moonbeam!" said Liam.

"Now all we have to do is get directions for Harper's Village."

Liam shook his head. "I know where it is. It's in the Dark Forest near where we met Gloria."

"You mean Little Red Riding Hood? It will take us at least a day to get there."

"Less if Otis can keep up the pace. You know, I really do like that horse."

CHAPTER 9

IT WAS GETTING DARK when Annie and Liam reached the grove of trees where they were going to spend the night. The grove was far enough off the road that passersby wouldn't bother them, but close enough that Otis nickered softly each time he heard another horse on the road. Liam kept watch while Annie slept. She didn't know if he dozed or not, but he was getting cold food out of his knapsack for their breakfast when she woke. They ate quickly and were soon on their way south.

A few hours later, they entered the Dark Forest. It was hilly ground, so they were constantly going up- or downhill as they followed curves in the road. Because there was little level ground and virtually no straightaways, they couldn't see very far ahead. Otis walked when the grade grew steeper, but he seemed to enjoy trotting downhill, so Liam let him have his head most of the time. They were rounding a downhill curve at a trot when they suddenly came upon a wagon stopped sideways across the road, blocking their way. When Liam turned Otis to the side to avoid running into the wagon, the horse tossed his head and Liam leaned back to avoid getting his face whacked. Something whizzed past, right where Liam's head had been, ruffling Otis's mane.

"What was that?" Annie asked as Otis danced to the side.

Before Liam could answer, an arrow whizzed past, narrowly missing Annie. "Someone is shooting arrows at us!" Liam cried, urging Otis off the road.

The horse floundered through the underbrush while Annie and Liam ducked to avoid the lower branches. A man appeared from behind a tree, forcing Otis to turn back. When another man appeared, Otis turned again and they found themselves back on the road before the curve.

"I hope you're up to this, boy," Liam said, patting Otis's neck, and then they were off at a gallop, hurtling through the curve, and heading straight for the wagon.

Both Liam and Annie had jumped horses before, and they knew when to shift their weight. As Otis flew over the wagon, Annie held on to Liam so tightly that it was almost as if one person rode the gelding. And then they were on the downward curve of the arc and Otis's hooves were creating a cloud of dust, leaving the highwaymen behind. The arrows that followed them missed their mark, but were enough to make Otis go faster. Up and down hills, over gulleys where rain had washed out the road, and under branches that could knock the unwary off a horse, the old gelding galloped as if his tail were on fire. When he finally began to slow, they were well into the Dark Forest and far from their pursuers.

Hearts racing and as out of breath as if they had been running themselves, Annie and Liam praised Otis, thankful that they had such a good horse under them. They made the horse walk to cool off, which gave them the chance to talk.

"Do you have any idea who those men were?" Annie asked Liam.

"None," he replied. "I got a good look at one of them, and I'd never seen him before. They were wearing ordinary clothes, too; nothing about them stood out."

"Do you think they know who we really are?"

"Either that or they were shooting at everyone who came along. Two farm boys on an old horse wouldn't be carrying enough money to make it worth their while. Say, I know where we are," said Liam. "See that lightning-blasted tree? If we turn here, we aren't far from the cottage where we first met Yardley."

"When he was a wolf," said Annie. "Yes, I remember."

"We could go there now and then on to Harper's Village," said Liam. "If anyone is following us, they wouldn't expect us to leave the road like this."

"That's a good idea," said Annie. "It will throw them off our track and we can see how Gloria's grandmother is doing."

Liam turned the horse toward the woods. "Not much farther and you can rest for a bit, Otis."

They rode for only a short while before dismounting and walking beside Otis. The gelding was exhausted from his gallop and walked slowly, stopping every now and then until Liam made him move again. They were finally approaching Little Red Riding Hood's grandmother's cottage when they heard the sound of someone chopping wood.

"It's probably Granny's son, the huntsman," said Annie. "I bet he came by to look in on her."

It wasn't the huntsman, but Yardley, the young man who had been turned into a wolf by a nasty dwarf. He was human again, thanks to Annie and Liam, who had hunted the dwarf down and given him a taste of his own magic.

"Yardley, what are you doing here?" Liam asked from the edge of the clearing that surrounded the cottage.

"Prince Liam, is that you? And who is that with you? Is that Princess Annie dressed like a boy again? You don't always dress that way, do you?"

"Not normally, at least not at home," Annie told him. "Why are you here? Where is Gloria's grandmother?"

"My wife and I bought the cottage from her. She didn't want to live in such an isolated spot any longer and moved in with one of her daughters." Setting down his ax, Yardley strode to the door and opened it, calling, "Honey! We have company."

Rose Red appeared in the doorway, smiling and wiping her hands on a rag. "Well, well! Would you look at what the wolf brought in! What are you two doing here? Beldegard isn't with you, is he?"

Annie shook her head. "He married my sister a few weeks ago. I don't think you'll be seeing much of him."

"I'd like to water the horse while we have the chance," Liam told Yardley. "Where is your well?"

"Right this way," said Yardley, and the two young men walked off with Otis.

"Would you like a cup of tea?" Rose Red asked Annie. "We don't have much, but we do have tea!"

"I'd love one!" said Annie, following Rose Red into the cottage. Taking a seat at the small table, she looked around the room while Rose Red moved from fireplace to table and back again. The cottage was cozy inside and was better laid out than it had been before. The bed no longer dominated the center of the room, but was pushed into a corner, with a table and chairs opposite and more chairs beside the fireplace. Annie recognized the cushions on the chairs as being like those she'd seen in Mother Hubbard's cottage. PEACE, HARMONY, HAPPINESS were written on three of the cushions and Annie could hear the faint magic that enforced the words.

"My mother gave me those pillows when I got married," said Rose Red. "They work, too. Yardley and I never have arguments when we're in the cottage. I never was serious about Beldegard, you know," said Rose Red as she set a mug in front of Annie. "Well, maybe I was for about fifteen minutes, but I didn't really think it would work out, him being a prince and all. I knew for sure when I saw him with your sister, the most beautiful princess in all the kingdoms. No, I've known for a while that the one I wanted to marry was Yardley. As soon as you turned him back into a human and he came home, he proposed to me. Mother made all the arrangements and we were married within a week. I can honestly say that I've never been happier."

"I'm happy for you," said Annie.

"That all happened right before your father locked away my mother's cousin," Rose Red told her. "Don't worry, no hard feelings. I never liked that side of the family anyway. When I was little I thought that Granny Bentbone was creepy. I wasn't surprised to hear that she ate children. Once, she told me that if I didn't behave she was going to turn me into a sausage. I believed her. My mother said that Granny Bentbone was joking, but it still gave me nightmares for weeks. Her daughter, Terobella, was even worse. She used to torture small animals for fun. I remember one time she was about to try some awful spell on me when my mother showed up. I made sure I was never alone with her after that. My mother said that her son was nicer, but he always went along with whatever his mother did, so I thought he was just as bad. When I heard that you turned Terobella into slime, I was sorry you hadn't turned him, too."

"I didn't really turn anyone into anything. She did it to herself."

"You know what I mean," said Rose Red.

"Tell me something," Annie said while Rose Red sipped her tea. "Your mother has some magic, and so does her cousin Granny Bentbone, but do you or your sister have any?"

Rose Red nodded. "A little, but not anything like Terobella. We can do some simple magic, like light fires and make water boil. Oh, and I can do illusions, although Snow White can't."

"What kind of illusions?" asked Annie.

"Nothing fancy," Rose Red replied. She glanced at the doorway and gestured. Suddenly a large gray wolf stood there, snarling. A moment later, the wolf was gone.

"Very good!" said Annie. If she hadn't heard the melody of the magic behind the illusion, she might have thought the wolf was real. "That must come in handy, being out here, just the two of you. I bet you could even scare off a bear with your illusions."

"Oh, I have," Rose Red said with a smile. "Tell me, why are you and Liam here? Looking for another dwarf?"

"A fairy, actually. We're hoping someone in Harper's Village might be able to tell us where we can find her."

"Is everything all right?" asked Rose Red.

Annie shook her head and was just about to speak when the door opened and Yardley came in with Liam close behind. "I hear people in the woods coming this way," Yardley told his wife. "Liam said that some men shot arrows at him and Annie. It's possible that these are the same people come to finish the job."

"You turned Yardley back into a human, but he still has exceptional hearing," his wife explained to Annie. "If he heard people, they're out there and will be here soon. You should leave now while I hold them off."

"I already told Liam how to get to Harper's Village from here," said Yardley.

"Are you sure you don't want me to stay and help?" Liam asked him. "I don't want to dump our troubles on you."

"No, no!" said Yardley. "We'll be fine. Rose Red and I have this handled."

"Then I guess we're leaving," Annie said, getting to her feet. "Thank you so much for the tea. It was just what I needed."

"You're welcome," Rose Red replied. "Stop in again whenever you're out this way. We hardly ever get to see anyone, and I enjoy the company."

Annie and Liam left then, going around to the back of the cottage to retrieve Otis from where he was tied to a tree. They had walked only a short distance when a loud roar made them stop and look behind them. A group of trolls were lumbering through the forest, retracing the route Annie and Liam had taken from the main road.

Liam's hand flew to his sword. "Where did they come from?" he demanded.

"From Rose Red's imagination would be my guess," said Annie. "Don't worry; they aren't real. I think they're meant to scare off the men following us."

"Rose Red did that?" said Liam. "But how?"

"Magic runs in her family, remember? She has a talent for illusions."

"Ah!" Liam said, putting his sword away. "That explains it. Yardley said they're never bored out here, or worried about intruders." They started walking again even as the trolls' roaring grew louder.

"Those men who are following us," said Annie. "They must know who we are or they wouldn't be so persistent."

Liam nodded. "I'm sure you're right."

"Do you think they're King Dormander's men? If they are, he must already know that we escaped from the castle."

"More than likely," Liam replied.

"You're not saying much."

"Sorry. I'm trying to figure out when they might have picked up our trail. Have they been following us since we left the castle? Maybe someone reported seeing us in the linder groves. Or did they learn about us in Floradale?"

"Eleanor's stepmother seemed to recognize us when we passed her on the street in Loralet. If she did, others probably did as well."

"Then we'd better hurry and find Moonbeam before anyone can stop us."

"I'm glad we're going to see her today," said Annie. "I'm tired of running around when all I want to do is go home and make sure everyone is all right. They're not going to be able to withstand a siege for long."

"I can't stop worrying about my father, too," said Liam. "The more I think about it, the more I doubt it was a coincidence that he didn't come to the wedding."

"Oh, Liam, I hope he's all right. Your father is too old and frail to be held captive by some army."

Liam laughed. "Don't let him hear you say that! Aside from his gout, he's as robust as ever, or at least he thinks he is."

"I like your father," said Annie.

"And he likes you," Liam said, smiling down at her. "But then, who wouldn't?"

"A lot of people, apparently. I don't think those men following us are any too fond of me. Say, I was wondering something. Did Yardley tell you why he and Rose Red decided to live so far from everything?"

"He did indeed," said Liam. "He wanted to live away from crowds for a while. Part of it was because he'd been a wolf and was afraid he wasn't acting fully human yet, and part of it was because a few of the men he played cards with were angry when he ran off with their money in the middle of a game. They didn't know the dwarf had turned him into a wolf and they've been looking for him ever since. He thought he and Rose Red would live here until things calm down a bit."

"I'm glad he did," said Annie. "Otherwise we'd be facing those men right now."

୫୭

It wasn't a very long walk to Harper's Village, but it was a pretty one. They passed through a grove of trees festooned with lacy white flowers and walked alongside a sparkling stream that tumbled down a small waterfall where they were able to refill the water skin and let Otis drink. A flock of bright red birds flew past them, startling Otis, but otherwise it was a very pleasant walk.

Before they entered the village, they saw at least three streets running parallel to one another and all of them looked busy. Annie was surprised that the village was so large. "This could almost be called a town," she told Liam as they walked down the main street, leading Otis. "Look at all the shops!"

"We're just here to find the butcher's son and talk to Moonbeam," said Liam. "We don't have time for anything else. Once we ask Moonbeam to go to Treecrest, we're going to go see my father."

"I know," said Annie, although she looked longingly at the inn they were passing. The smell of roasting beef was almost enough to make her stop.

A short time later, they walked by a cobbler who was working on a bench outside his shop, taking advantage of the good weather. "Pardon me," Annie said as she stopped in front of him, "but do you know where we can find Jamesey Dunlop?"

"Never heard of him," the man replied, looking annoyed.

"We need to ask someone else," Annie told Liam as they walked away. "Someone less surly."

"Gertrude said that her brother started his own shop, so we should look for a butcher. It shouldn't be too hard. The village isn't *that* big."

The aroma of freshly baked bread wafting from a bakery slowed Annie's steps. "Is it my imagination, or does this village smell better than most?" she asked, taking another deep breath.

"You're hungry and that bread does smell good. I suppose it wouldn't hurt to get something to eat," said Liam.

He hadn't finished his sentence before Annie was opening the door to the bakery. It was warm and even more fragrant inside. A girl in a white cap and apron was helping customers while two other people worked in the back, taking bread out of a huge brick oven and decorating a pastry shaped like a swan. There were three people in line to buy bread ahead of Annie. She fidgeted, shifting her weight from one foot to the other as the shopgirl waited on the other customers. When it was finally her turn, Annie looked at the girl more closely. "Gloria! I didn't recognize you without your red hood."

"Do I know you?" Gloria asked, peering at Annie. "Wait, you're one of the people who scared the wolf out of Granny's house! What are you doing in Harper's Village?"

"Looking for someone," said Annie. "Do you know where I can find Jamesey Dunlop's butcher shop?"

"Do I ever! He married my cousin and I work there some days when I'm not working here. I'd take you there myself, but I can't leave the bakery now. His shop is located on the next street over. Go to the corner and turn left. His shop is on the opposite side of the street. Harper's Village has grown a lot lately, and that's where the newest shops are."

"It looks like a prosperous village," said Annie.

"Oh, it is! I have a big family and they've all stayed here, and lots of other people have started moving here as well. I love Harper's Village! Everyone knows everyone else."

"Really? I asked a cobbler if he knew where I could find Jamesey Dunlop and he said he didn't know him."

"That would be my uncle Nick. He knows Jamesey, but he probably just didn't feel like talking to you. He's been crotchety ever since he gave some clothes to the brownies who were helping him and they left for good. Now he has to do all the work himself and he's always falling behind."

"He did look annoyed when I spoke to him. Oh, while I'm here I wanted to get something to eat."

"Try our hot cross buns," said Gloria. "They're really good. I helped make them myself."

"How much do I owe you?" Annie asked as Gloria handed her the buns.

"Nothing," said the girl. "You helped my whole family when you chased off that wolf. One of my older brothers owns the bakery and I know he wouldn't want me to charge you anything. In fact, if there's ever anything we can do to help you, just let us know. We owe you for helping me the way you did."

"You already did help," said Annie. "You told me where to find the butcher. Thanks for the directions and the buns!" With a wave of her hand, Annie was out the door and handing one of the buns to Liam.

"I know where the butcher is located," she said before taking a big bite.

Liam stepped to the side as Otis tried to snuffle his hair. "Oh, really! Where?"

Annie's mouth was already full, so she just pointed to the corner, then indicated that they should turn there.

"And how did you learn this?"

She chewed quickly and swallowed the bite before saying, "I asked Gloria, of course. I told you we should ask someone."

Following Gloria's directions, they found the butcher shop easily. The entire area smelled of fresh wood shavings, and Annie could see that many of the buildings were new. While Annie opened the shop door, Liam tied Otis to a post. The only person inside was a short young man with a round belly and thick brown hair. Seeing them at the door, he smiled and gestured for them to come in. "How can I help you today?" he asked. "I have some excellent pork chops if you're interested."

"That sounds very nice, but we're actually looking for someone," said Annie. "We understand that your father and your new stepmother came to visit you. Could we talk to Moonbeam, please?"

The young man lost his smile the moment Annie mentioned Moonbeam. "They aren't here anymore, thank goodness. I had more than enough of that woman, er . . . fairy . . . whatever!"

"Isn't she kind to you?" asked Annie.

"Oh, no, she's very nice to me and to my sisters, trying to make up for everything she's done. She's always giving us presents because she knows she's destroying our lives. And the way she treats my father! She has him wrapped around her little finger. He'll do anything she asks, even if it means putting his own children out into the cold."

"He kicked you out?"

"In a sense. She made him tell us that we had to get jobs and take responsibility for our lives. Can you believe it? And then she had my father tell me that I had to marry the girl I'd been seeing for the past two years. I'd told him often enough that I would get around to it when I was ready, but oh, no! He had to push it. So I married Dorothea and moved here, where her family lives. Father had changed so much, I couldn't stand to be around him anymore, and Dorothea's family does what every family is supposed to do. They're there when we need them and leave us alone the rest of the time."

"Sounds just right for you," said Annie.

"You said that Moonbeam and your father left. Can you tell us where they went?" Liam asked.

"They went to visit a friend of hers. A fairy with a dumb name. I think it was Sweetness at Night."

"Do you mean Sweetness N Light?" asked Annie.

"Yeah, that's it. 'Good riddance,' I said as soon as they were out the door. I hope they don't come back for a good long time."

"I have one other question, if you don't mind," said Liam. "How were you able to get a shop of your own? I mean, you aren't that old. Wasn't it expensive?"

Jamesey shrugged. "It was, but my father and Moonbeam paid for it, which was only right. After all, they were the ones who made me leave home!"

CHAPTER 10

AFTER THANKING THE BUTCHER, Liam untied Otis from the post and helped Annie onto the gelding's back. They rode in silence for a time with both of them lost in thought. When they reached the first crossroad, Liam reined in Otis. "Before we go east to the Garden of Happiness, I want to head south and see how my father is doing. We're only a few hours away and it doesn't make sense to go all the way to the garden, then come back here when we're so close now."

"But didn't you just say that we had to hurry to find Moonbeam? We have all those people counting on us back at the castle!"

"And my father may be in real trouble here in Dorinocco. I understand it's urgent that we find Moonbeam, but I need to make sure that my father is all right. Please understand, Annie. I wouldn't do this unless I felt it was necessary."

"I know," Annie said. She felt so torn, she wasn't sure what to do. She knew how important it was that they find Moonbeam, but what if King Montague was in trouble as well? And Liam was right, they were very close. "All right. It shouldn't take long if we're only a few hours away. We'll go to the castle, see that he's fine, and go on to the garden."

"Thank you, Annie," Liam said.

Annie hadn't realized how worried he was that she wouldn't agree until she felt the tension leave him and heard the relief in his voice. Sighing, she leaned against him, resting her head on his back and hugging him. "You know I'll always be there for you."

"And I'll always be there for you," he said, pressing her hand with his own. "I just didn't want to make you go with me if you didn't want to, but I really have to do this."

Liam turned Otis onto the road heading south and let the gelding set his own pace. The horse had gotten his second wind and moved along with his ears pricked forward, interested in seeing what lay ahead. Annie and Liam rode in silence then, while Annie worried about what might be happening at home, and wondered if they had made the right decision. They were only a few miles from the castle when a patrol wearing King Montague's colors passed them by.

"Why didn't they greet you?" Annie asked. "They all looked right at us, but not one of them seemed to recognize you, their crown prince."

"I've never seen any of them before," Liam said, sounding puzzled. "I thought I knew all of my father's men."

"Perhaps they're new," said Annie.

"All of them? That doesn't make sense. He's never taken on that many new men all at once. I'll have to ask him about it when we see him."

They had been on the main road leading to the castle for only a short time when Liam muttered something to himself. "What did you say?" asked Annie.

"Something isn't right," he repeated in a louder voice. "There should be traffic on this stretch of the road, but we haven't passed anyone other than that patrol. I don't like this."

"We're almost there," said Annie. "We'll find out what's going on soon enough."

They reached the castle a few minutes later. Although it was only late afternoon, the drawbridge was up and they didn't see anyone on the parapet. "Do you hear that?" asked Liam.

"What?" said Annie. "I don't hear anything."

Liam nodded. "Exactly! The courtyard is usually full of people this time of day, and it's so loud you can hear it from this side of the wall. There should be guards out here and people waiting in line to cross over the drawbridge, but no one is here and it's quiet. Something is definitely not right."

"What do you want to do?" asked Annie.

"See who comes out." Cupping his hands around his mouth, he threw back his head and shouted, "Hello, the gate!"

After what seemed like a very long time, a man appeared on the parapet to look down at them. "What do you want?" he said in a rude voice.

"Is Godfrey there, or Thurmont?"

"No one here by either of those names. Go away and stop wasting my time. You can't come in no matter who you know. Can't you see that the drawbridge is closed?"

"It's awfully early in the day for that," said Liam.

"No one asked for your opinion! Go away if you know what's good for you."

Annie was incredulous when Liam turned the horse and rode away. "I can't believe he talked to you like that!"

"He has no idea who I am," Liam told her. "I have a feeling that if he did, we would have gotten a very different and highly unpleasant reception. I don't know who he is, either, but I do know that neither Godfrey nor Thurmont would let a new recruit handle the drawbridge by himself. And if he doesn't even know their names . . . something is definitely wrong here."

"Where are we going?"

"To find someone who should be able to answer a few questions," said Liam.

They rode away from the castle, heading toward the town of Casaway, but they had only just caught sight of it when Liam turned Otis onto a side road.

"I thought we were going to the town," said Annie.

"We were until I saw a group of mounted men posted on the street just outside. As far as I could see, they weren't wearing uniforms, but they sat their horses like military men and are probably there to question new arrivals. I'd prefer to avoid being questioned, so we're going somewhere else."

The road took them between an apple orchard and a hayfield before crossing over a stone bridge and the sparkling brook below. "This is the Old Stone Bridge," said Liam. He pointed at a run-down shack yards from the base of the bridge. "And that is Meckle's house. Godfrey is his son. I met Meckle when I was just a lad. He's a good man, although he's getting up in years and tends to repeat himself."

"He lives alone here?" Annie asked, eyeing the shack with distrust. "It looks as if it's about to fall down." All four walls were leaning and the roof was sagging so badly that she wondered how anyone could walk around inside. An old dog that was missing half an ear lifted his head from the ground he was lying on, gave a halfhearted woof, then laid his head down again as if it was too heavy to hold up.

"It's looked like that for years, but he refuses to let anyone fix it. Don't worry, we won't be going in. Meckle prefers to entertain outside."

While Annie held the rope and let Otis nibble the grass by the foot of the bridge, Liam knocked on the cobbled-together door. A few seconds later an old man shorter than Annie threw the door open to glare at them. He had to be the oldest man Annie had ever seen. Sparse white hair surrounded a bald patch on the crown of his head. His face was a map of wrinkles, and his eyes were a watery blue.

"Do I know you?" the man asked, his voice surprisingly deep. He eyed Annie and turned to Liam before studying Otis for just as long.

"It's me, Liam," said the prince, keeping his voice down.

"Liam who?" asked Meckle.

"You know—Prince Liam," Liam said in a fierce whisper.

The old man peered up at Liam for just a second before saying, "Nope, can't be. Prince Liam is in Treecrest getting married. Just as well, considering what's going on at the castle."

"What's going on?" asked Liam.

"Don't know. Nobody does. Drawbridge has been up for the last five days. Did I tell you my son came to see me six days ago? Good boy, my Godfrey. Always checking up on me. Promised to bring me eggs the next day, but he never did bring 'em. Not like my Godfrey at all. I taught him if you make a promise, you darn well better keep it. When he didn't come by the day after that, either, I put on my shoes and walked over there. Thought he might have caught some sort of ailment. Never did see him, though. Drawbridge was up. The fool posted there wouldn't tell me what was going on. I'd taught half the boys in that castle how to fish and catch crawdads in that creek," the old man said, nodding toward the stream behind his shack. "Prince Liam, too." He gave Liam a meaningful look. "But not that fool. Never seen him before, nor any of the others riding around in packs making nuisances of 'emselves."

"And none of your friends have been inside the castle?" asked Liam. "What about food deliveries?"

Meckle shrugged. "No idea. For all I know they could be conjuring up food with magic." He laughed so hard that his little potbelly bounced. "Imagine that! I'd like to try that one myself."

"It sounds as if someone is hiding something in the castle," said Liam.

"Seems that way," the old man replied, wiping tears from his eyes.

"If we were to leave our horse here for a few hours, would you take care of him?" Liam asked him. "Make sure that no one steals him and that he's fed and watered? I'll see you get those eggs you wanted if you'll do that for me."

"Well, young man who claims to be Prince Liam, let me give you some advice. Don't tell anyone what you told me. If Prince Liam really was here, people would be looking for him, and not to do him any favors. Leave your horse. I know of an out-of-the-way pasture where he can eat alfalfa till he's fat as a tick and no one to bother him. And I'll take those eggs. No saying when my boy will be bringing any to me now."

After handing Otis's rope to the old man, Annie and Liam were walking away when Meckle called after them. "If you happen to find a way in, check on my boy if you would. I'd help him myself, but my bones are too stiff for climbing."

Liam nodded and waved back, which seemed to satisfy the old man.

"What did he mean by climbing?" Annie asked as they headed toward the stream.

"I grew up in this castle and I know it better than anyone, inside and out. When I was a lad, I told only one person about some of the secret passages I'd found, and that was Meckle. He may be old and pretending not to know me, but he knew exactly who I was and what I plan to do."

"But climbing?" said Annie.

Liam laughed. "Don't worry. It won't be up the side of a tower or castle wall. We'll be climbing some steep stairs and going places no one has gone for a very long time to find out what those men don't want anyone to know."

Instead of crossing over the bridge, they walked along the stream bank, heading back toward the castle. "Why are we going this way?" asked Annie.

"We'll approach the castle from a different direction, one that no one ever watches," said Liam. "This stream goes through the woods and loops behind the castle. I used to follow this path a lot when I was a child. Anything to get out of the castle and away from my mother and brother. That's how I got to know Meckle."

"Your brother didn't play out here as well?"

"Clarence spent all his time in the castle. Mother was always pampering him, so he already had everything he ever wanted."

They followed the stream through the woods, crossing to the other side in the narrowest part of a loop, then creeping through the trees and around the side of the castle to a vast and smelly pit nearly full of refuse. The castle rose high above them, and Annie could see from the discolored stones exactly where people dumped the trash out of openings in the walls.

"This place reeks!" she said, holding her nose.

"It smells worse in the middle of summer when it's hot out. I'm thankful that it does smell bad. The stench is the reason this is such a good spot to sneak in. No one wants to breathe this if they can help it."

Annie tilted her head back to look up at the castle. "You said we didn't have to climb the wall. So how are we getting in?"

"Through the door," Liam said. "Follow me." He led her along the base of the wall, around the biggest piles of refuse, to a shadowed niche that she didn't see until they were close. "This was probably used when the castle was newly built, but no one had used it in years when I found it. I actually discovered the door from the inside, then had to work my way along the outside wall until I located the door buried behind old trash. I was interested in finding ways out of the castle because I never knew when my mother would decide to take out her bad mood on me. Stand back while I clear the space in front of the door so we can open it. I left a shovel here for that very reason. Ah, there we are. Stay here while I find the torch. I know I left a few just inside."

Annie waited while Liam slipped into the dark interior of the castle. She could hear him bumping into things and knocking things over. When she heard rustling behind her, she turned in surprise and spotted a large rat nosing through the garbage not five feet away. Her eye caught more movement and she realized that there were rats everywhere, scurrying from pile to pile, gnawing on bits and pieces of things. Spotting a medium-size rat watching her, she edged closer to the door.

The rat was motionless except for its twitchy little nose. Suddenly a big black snake shot out of an opening in the trash and swallowed the rat whole. A moment later, the snake flowed from the first opening into a gap a few feet away. Although Annie never saw it exposed all at once, she noted that it was as big around as her wrist and seemed to go on forever. She edged even closer to the door.

"Found it!" Liam said as he emerged holding an unlit torch. Taking a flint from his knapsack, he lit the torch and gestured toward the door. "Now we can see what everyone is trying to hide."

Chapter 11

ANNIE WAS GETTING USED to walking through narrow passages with only torchlight to show the way, although she didn't like it. After climbing stairs that were so steep and shallow that the toes of her shoes barely fit on the step, she was glad to be on a level floor again.

She almost tripped over Liam when he stopped suddenly and bent down to lift a stone out of the floor, revealing a hole as big as his fist. "What is that?" she asked.

"This looks down through the ceiling in the great hall. You can't see much from here, but it's surprising how much you can hear. Hold on. Let me listen."

Liam held his ear close to the opening for nearly a minute before he sat back and shook his head. "It seems there's nothing to hear—no talking or footsteps or snoring or anything. I don't think anyone is down there, which is very unusual. Let's go check the kitchen."

They descended another narrow set of stairs and reached a short corridor that smelled strongly of old smoke and stale food. Annie found the skeleton of a dead rat in the middle of the floor and stepped around it. When she heard a scraping sound, she thought it was another rat, but it was Liam taking the cover off a tiny peephole. Pressing his face to the wall, Liam peered into the kitchen. Annie held her breath and heard the faint sound of metal banging against metal.

"What did you see?" she asked when he closed the peephole.

"A guard rooting through the pots and pans. I heard someone else moving around, too, so there were at least two of them."

"Could I get to look sometime? Even if there isn't much to see," said Annie.

"Oh, sure. Sorry! We'll go back upstairs now and see if my father is in his room."

They walked for what seemed like miles, climbing more stairs and following paths that zigged and zagged around oddly shaped rooms, public stairwells, and hidden niches. They passed outlines of doors cut into the walls as well as peepholes and sliding panels, both large and small. Annie felt as if Liam was giving her a tour of all the secret passages in his father's castle, but she was certain he had a destination in mind.

They were walking down yet another narrow, dust-filled corridor when Annie sneezed. The dust they stirred up tickled her nose and throat, and she sneezed again and again.

"Shh!" Liam whispered. "We have to be extra-quiet through here. There are bedchambers on either side of us."

Annie fought to get her sneezing under control. She pinched her nose and held her breath until her eyes watered. When she didn't sneeze again, she gave Liam a weak smile, took a shallow breath, and coughed. "It's the dust," she said. "Sorry."

Liam took his knapsack off his back and reached inside. "Here, we'll tie this over your face. It might cut down on the dust."

Annie held her breath while he tied a clean hand-kerchief just under her eyes, knotting it behind her head. "I feel like a bandit," she said when he was done. "Wearing a mask and lurking behind the walls."

"Prettiest bandit anywhere," Liam said, kissing her cloth-covered nose. "Now watch and learn. This is my father's room. I can tell by the mark I made on the wall years ago. Let's see if he's in."

Annie looked at the circle with the star drawn on the wall next to a full-size outline of a door. She thought Liam was going to open the door, but instead he stepped about three feet to his left and slid a small panel to the side. After peering through the opening for a moment, he moved aside, saying, "No one is in there, but you can take a look if you'd like."

Annie peeked into the room. From where she stood, she could see part of the drapes that surrounded the bed, a sizeable cabinet, and a small table with a single chair. As far as she could tell, nothing was moving in the room and the only sounds she could hear were her own breathing and heartbeat.

"You're right," she told Liam as she slid the panel shut. "There's no one there."

"I've never heard silence like this before," said Liam. "There's usually some noise even in the middle of the night."

"Now you know what it was like when Gwennie touched the spinning wheel and everybody in the castle fell asleep except me," said Annie. "There were people everywhere, yet I never felt so alone in my life." She turned from the panel to the outline of the door. "Why is there a panel here when there is already a door into the room?"

"As far as I can figure out, these passages were built into the castle for the first king of Dorinocco. He probably used the door to go places in secret. The panel was probably put in so he could make sure no one, like the queen or even a maid cleaning his room, was there when he returned."

"Ah," said Annie. "So why were there doors and panels to other rooms?"

"I suppose it was so he could spy on everyone else, or visit people without anyone else knowing."

"He sounds very sneaky," said Annie.

"Or very shrewd," Liam said as he glanced down the length of the passageway. "Let's check some of the other rooms. You take that side and I'll take this one."

Annie nodded. Reluctant to spy on people and invade their privacy, she was nervous and slid the first panel aside slowly and carefully. She held her breath as she peeked inside, but it was just another furniture-filled room with no one in it. Moving on to the next, she slid it aside more quickly and found a nearly identical room. While Liam peered into one room after another, Annie took her time. After checking a few rooms, she began to think that none of them were occupied and she and Liam were wasting their time.

Annie and Liam both looked up when they heard the faint sound of a door slam somewhere nearby. "Sounds like someone isn't in a good mood," Liam whispered. "Let's see if we can find out why."

They heard voices then, muted by the wall, but still distinguishable as the higher-pitched voice of a woman and the lower pitch of a man. Moving as quietly as they could, Annie and Liam located the room by following the voices. The panel covering the opening to the room was set back in a little alcove. The dust was thicker there, tickling Annie's nose despite the handkerchief. She looked up when she heard Liam's indrawn breath.

"This is my mother's room," whispered Liam. "See the mark on the wall?" Annie nodded when she spotted the circle with an *X* through it that marked the door. "This means she got out of the tower somehow. Whatever is going on here, she must be behind it."

The voices were louder now, as if the people inside were shouting, but Annie still couldn't make out what they were saying. When Liam slid the panel aside, Annie stepped closer. "It *is* my mother," Liam breathed as he peeked into the room. "And Clarence! My dear brother is back from his travels in time to cause trouble. I should have guessed."

"Shh! Let's listen!" whispered Annie.

"It isn't right!" the queen complained to her son Clarence. "I should never have promised the wizard that I'd stay in the castle until his return. Now his men think they have the right to keep me here. And it isn't at all the way I thought it would be. You said that Dormander's wizard would help him take over Treecrest in days, but he still isn't back!"

"He's a very powerful wizard," said Clarence. "They're probably on their way back now."

"Powerful, you say? Then why did the spell he cast on everyone last only a day?"

"Everyone but us, Mother," said Clarence. "You know I wouldn't let him use his magic on us."

"I know, dear boy, and everything would have been fine if the spell had lasted as long as he promised.

The wizard told us that everyone will think we're the rightful rulers. 'They'll turn on Montague and lock him in the dungeon,' he said. And then he left and a day later the spell started wearing off and we had to make the last few loyal guards lock everyone in the dungeon, then lock themselves in as well before *they* remembered the truth. Now we have no servants to cook or clean."

"But that guard—"

"Don't you dare tell me again that the guard who took over the cooking is doing a decent job, because he isn't! The fish last night was burned and not at all fresh. I'm surprised it didn't give me stomach issues. To think I don't even have any ladies-in-waiting to help me dress, or courtiers to entertain me, and the only guards who aren't locked away are the few men the wizard left here. And those guards won't let us leave even though we ordered them to. I'm a prisoner in my own home! I need a bath and a decent meal. Going down to the dungeon to talk to your father is my only entertainment, and he hasn't been pleasant to me in years. I was better off locked in the tower, Clarence. I'm not saying I don't want you home, because I'm delighted that you're back, but did you have to bring that wizard with you?"

"I met him at the seaport when they were boarding their ships," said Clarence. "When he learned who I was, he insisted on bringing me back. It wasn't as if I had any say in the matter. Besides, I was sure he would help our cause."

"He and his king are probably helping themselves to Treecrest and leaving us here to rot," the queen declared.

Liam's mother was no longer shouting, and Annie found it harder to hear her. She took a step closer to the wall, stirring up more dust. Feeling the tickle in her nose, she clapped her hand over her face and tried her best not to sneeze, but it came out anyway in a short, sharp, slightly strangled sound.

"What was that?" asked Clarence even as Liam slid the panel shut.

"Sorry!" Annie whispered to Liam.

"It's all right," he whispered back. "We heard enough. I know where everyone is and what we have to do now."

Liam strode to the closest set of stairs, walking so quickly that Annie had to run to keep up. They went down the stairs, along another passage, then down two more sets of stairs, including the one with the shallow steps that Annie hated. As soon as they reached the last step, Liam turned left and walked a short distance to what looked like a solid wall. Running his hands across the surface of the wall, he found a small protrusion and moved it down a few inches. Rock groaned and a door opened. The torchlight wavered as damp air washed over them. They were in an old section of the dungeon now, where the bars on the windows and the hinges on the doors were rusty from moisture. Liam led the way again, and before long Annie heard voices. There were people here, and they didn't sound happy.

"Let us out!" shouted an older man. "You have it all wrong! We shouldn't be here."

"Why do you bother?" asked a voice that Annie recognized as Liam's father's. "There's no one down here but our own people."

"I heard something. I thought one of the guards had come back."

Liam hurried down the corridor, heading for the cell where his father was still talking. "Even if a guard was here, he wouldn't help us," said King Montague.

"But I will," Liam said, peering through the small barred window in the cell door. "Is everyone all right?"

"Liam! It's good to see you," said the king. "We're hungry and dirty, but fine otherwise."

"They brought us gruel once a day," called a voice. "I'm sick of it! And to think I used to like gruel!"

"I didn't know anyone liked gruel," said a voice farther down the corridor.

"Annie, wait here while I get the keys," said Liam. "They should be hanging on a hook at the other end of the hall."

Annie watched the torchlight shrink as Liam moved down the corridor, but he was soon back to open the doors. He let his father out first as well as the guards locked in with him. There were five, including

Godfrey and Thurmont, two of the guards she'd met before. While Annie spoke to the king, Liam moved down the row, opening one door after another until all of the prisoners had been freed.

"Do you know what Dormander's wizard did?" asked Liam's father.

Liam nodded. "I heard Mother talking to Clarence. Does anyone have any idea how many of the wizard's guards are in the castle?"

"Six," said a young woman. "I know because I work in the kitchen and had to take them their meals."

"You might want to stay down here while I go upstairs with some of your men," Liam told his father. "This shouldn't take us very long if there are only six guards. Annie, would you mind staying with my father?"

"But—" Annie began.

"It will be much easier for me if I know that the two people I love most in the world are safe," said Liam.

"If you put it that way," said Annie.

While Liam led the guards upstairs, his father told Annie what it had been like to be locked in his own dungeon. "It wouldn't have been so bad if my gout hadn't been acting up when they locked me down here. It's better now, though. I wonder if an all-gruel diet helped."

They were discussing the different things you could do to gruel to make it tastier when Liam and the guards returned, bringing all six of the wizard's men with them. "We fought one guard and the rest gave in," said Liam as King Montague's guards walked their new prisoners to the cells. "We would have been back sooner, but we had to lock Mother and Clarence in the tower. It was odd; she was waiting in her chamber almost as if she expected us to come for her."

"She did say she was better off before Clarence came back. Maybe she just wanted it to be over," said Annie.

"Is it all right if we go upstairs and get to work?" asked a middle-aged woman.

"Please!" someone shouted. "Let her go!"

"Yes, she should go first!" someone else called out.

"Of course," said Liam. "It should be safe now."

"Who was that?" Annie asked as the woman bustled up the steps.

"The head cook," said the old guard named Godfrey. "We can't wait for something decent to eat for a change."

"Did you get married yet, my dear?" the old king asked Annie as they started toward the stairs. "I'm so sorry I missed it if you did."

"No, we had a bit of trouble and had to postpone it, but we do intend to have the wedding soon," said Annie. "We'll send word when we've rescheduled. Liam, perhaps we should spend the night here. It's already getting late and we'd have to stop soon anyway."

133

"Good idea," said Liam. "But before I turn in for the night, there are a few things I have to do. The castle kitchen is probably short of supplies, so I won't bother the cook for eggs, but can someone suggest where I can purchase a dozen or so? I have a debt to repay and a horse to claim so we can get an early start in the morning."

CHAPTER 12

ANNIE AND LIAM WERE WAITING when the drawbridge was lowered at dawn the next morning. Liam had taken a stallion named Hunter from his father's stable, but Annie had refused when he'd offered her a fresh horse as well. She liked Otis and intended to ride him the rest of the way home, although she had accepted a new bridle and saddle. Well fed and rested from his visit with Meckle and a night in a royal stall, Otis was in a good mood. His ears pricked forward with interest when the creaking of the chains finally stopped and the drawbridge hit the ground with a thump.

A line of wagons on the other side of the drawbridge were waiting to come in. Annie glanced at the wagons as Otis trotted past them. From what she could see, word of what had happened had already spread and the citizens of the kingdom had responded with fresh produce, jugs of cream-rich milk, wheels of cheese, and a variety of meats and fish. Seeing all the people arriving on horseback, she was sure that the curious had also come to visit.

Once on their way, Annie and Liam rode side by side in companionable silence. They were just about to enter the Dark Forest when something occurred to Annie.

"Your mother's name is Lenore, right?" she said to Liam.

"Hmm?" he murmured. "Oh, yes, that's right."

"Well, so is Eleanor's stepmother. Named Lenore, I mean."

"You're right," Liam replied. "It's appropriate, don't you think? They're both awful mothers who favor certain children and hold others in contempt. I'm sure my mother would have turned me into a servant if it had occurred to her."

"Your father would never have allowed it!" said Annie.

Liam chuckled. "Well, there is that. Thank goodness for good fathers!"

Suddenly, Otis tossed his head and snorted. A tiny finch had landed on his forelock and was clinging to the hair with its talons even as the horse tried to shake it off. Chirping madly, the finch stared up at Annie, getting louder when she didn't respond. Finally, it gave an extra-loud chirp and flew from Otis to Hunter.

"Hello! Hello! Can you hear me now?" chirped the finch. "I've been calling to you for ever so long."

"Look, Liam!" said Annie. "I think it's the finch that we freed from the ogre's cage."

"No time to talk!" chirped the finch. "You're in big trouble—"

"Is that really the same bird?" Liam asked.

"Yes, it's me!" the bird chirped, managing to sound annoyed. "Will you be quiet and listen? The girl set me free, so I followed her. Somebody is good to you, you should be good back. I've been watching over her."

"A talking bird. We probably shouldn't trust it. Remember that talking fish?" asked Liam.

"Just because the fish was a liar doesn't mean the bird will be, too. You said there was trouble?" Annie prompted the finch.

"Yes! Some bad men are following you. They have been ever since your horse almost tripped over that wagon."

"We knew they followed us to Yardley's cottage," Annie said to Liam.

"The not-real trolls scared them away," said the finch. "Then the men went to that bunch of houses and asked about you. Someone told them which way you went. The road split and so did they. The ones that went to the big house wouldn't have caught up if you hadn't stayed there last night."

"You mean the castle," said Liam.

137

"I don't know what *you* call it," replied the finch.

"Where are these men now?" Annie asked the finch.

"Behind you. They're riding with some families who are going this way. I heard them talking. They plan to attack you in the woods after the families ride on. You might want to ask your horses to go a little faster."

Annie and Liam glanced back the way they had come. A large group was riding up behind them, but they were too far away to see their faces.

"Good idea, bird," said Liam. "We can lose them in the forest."

"Thank you for telling us," Annie told the finch.

"I haven't finished helping you," said the finch. "You saved my life. All I did was tell you something. See you later!"

Annie watched the finch fly off into the Dark Forest. She was about to ask Otis to go faster when Liam reached out and put his hand on top of hers. "Not yet. We'll wait until those men can't see us. No need to get them to hurry now. And don't look back," he added when she started to turn around. "We don't want them to know that we know they're there."

Annie nodded, but she was impatient to get away from the men, so as soon as she and Liam were out of sight among the trees, she urged Otis to break into a gallop. With Hunter galloping beside Otis, they kept going until they had put a good distance between themselves and their pursuers, then slowed to look for a side road that Liam remembered having traveled years before. That road took them only partway before they were looking for another.

They had angled back and forth heading northwest for some time when Liam stopped to look around. "Are we lost?" Annie asked, although she wasn't really worried. One of the few fairy-given christening gifts Liam had received had been an impeccable sense of direction. Unfortunately, it worked only when he wasn't near Annie.

"Just a minute." Liam rode off a short distance and sat looking in every direction. "It's that way," he said a moment later, turning his horse.

It took them only a few hours to reach the bank of the Crystal River across from the town of Farley's Crossing, where the only ferry on the river was located. Unfortunately, the ferry wasn't there, but they could see it docked on the opposite bank.

"Look, people are lining up to get on," said Annie. "They should be here soon."

Liam's expression was grim. "I hope so. If those men take the roads, they'll be here in a few hours. I don't want to be stuck on this side when they arrive."

"I'll go see where they are," said the finch.

"I didn't know she was still with us," Annie said as the little bird flew off.

"I didn't, either," said Liam. "How do you know it's a she?"

"Her drab brown feathers," Annie replied. "A male would have brighter colors. One of the stable boys taught me about birds years ago. I guess it's good that we didn't notice her. That means those men probably won't either."

"She is proving to be more useful than I thought," said Liam. "It will help to know where those men are."

While they waited for the ferry, Annie and Liam dismounted and let their horses nibble the grass along the riverbank. They watched as people boarded the ferry, waiting with growing impatience while the ferrymen took their time getting started. An elderly man and his three adult daughters joined Annie and Liam on their side of the river, forming their own line behind them. When the ferry finally arrived, Annie and Liam had to wait for the passengers to disembark.

Annie and Liam were leading their horses toward the ferry, planning to get on, when the old ferryman in charge held up his hand and shook his head. "Not yet, folks. If we sit a spell, more passengers are bound to show up. Even if they don't, my men need a break before we go back."

"And how long do you expect this break to last?" asked Liam.

The ferryman gave him a sour look. "As long as it needs to. If you don't like it, you can go the long way around."

"Or your men could take their break after they give us a ride across and earn some extra money doing it," Liam said, flipping a gold coin in the air and catching it.

"Or they could do that," the ferryman said, his fingers twitching as if he'd wanted to catch the coin.

Everything happened quickly then. Annie and Liam walked their horses on with the elderly man and his daughters trailing behind. As soon as they were on board, the ferrymen began hauling them across the river. They were part of the way across when Annie glanced back, wondering what had become of the little finch.

Although Otis didn't seem to mind the ride, the bouncing and shaking of the ferry and the slapping of the waves against its side made Hunter restless. One of the women's horses on the back of the ferry was so agitated that Annie was afraid it was going to hurt someone; she was glad when they reached the other side without incident.

The moment they stopped, the old ferryman held out his hand. Liam tossed him the gold coin as he walked Hunter onto the dock, mounting up once they were on dry land. Annie and Otis followed them to shore, and they rode through Farley's Crossing side by side. They were passing the Gasping Guppy when the finch landed on Liam's arm.

"Did you see the men?" asked Liam.

"I did," said the finch. "They won't be following you anytime soon. I flew into the face of one of the horses.

It got scared and stood on its back legs and dumped its rider off. The other horse got scared, too, and tripped over a log. It's lame now and the man who fell off his horse is very sore. But they aren't the ones you should worry about. The two men who went the other way are here now. They saw you get off the ferry. They're waiting just down the street."

"Good to know," said Liam. "Thank you!"

"This is fun!" said the finch. "I've never done anything like this before."

"What do you want to do?" Annie asked Liam. "Ride fast through town or try to evade them?"

"Evade, then ride fast," said Liam. "We'll go this way first."

Turning left, they rode between the Gasping Guppy and the stable next door. After rounding the back of the stable, they rode through the trees and underbrush that defined the edge of town, returning to the road only after they were well past Farley's Crossing.

Annie had no idea how to reach the Garden of Happiness from this direction, but Liam knew precisely where to go. They had been there before, and Liam could find his way anywhere he had visited at least once.

CHAPTER 13

THE SKY WAS GROWING DARK earlier than Annie had expected when she looked up to see clouds gathering overhead. "It's going to rain," she told Liam. "Do you think we'll reach the garden soon?"

"If we had a road to take us straight there, probably. As it is, we'll have to spend the night in the forest. We should try to find shelter before the rain begins," Liam said, giving the sky an appraising look. "The wind is picking up. It looks as if we're heading into a storm."

Annie was startled when the finch landed on her arm. She chirped at Annie, but when she gave her a blank look, the little bird left and flew to Liam. "Why can't I talk like a human when I land on the girl?" the bird asked him.

"Because magic doesn't work near me," Annie answered for Liam.

"Oh," said the finch. "I'll try to remember that. I came to tell you that those men are behind you. They've been on your trail for a while now. I didn't see him before, but there must have been another one waiting outside of that bunch of houses. He's with them now. I think he told them that you'd gone past."

"They probably don't want to show themselves until dark," said Liam. "Let's see if we can lose them."

They rode faster then, staying on the road for as long as they could. Annie was hoping that they had already lost the men when one of the horses following them whinnied. Although Otis didn't respond, Hunter screamed back.

"One of those men must be riding a mare in heat," said Liam. "I should never have chosen a stallion." When it happened again a few miles down the road, Liam jerked on the reins and muttered under his breath.

It started to rain and Annie expected Liam to want to find shelter, but he seemed more intent on distancing them from their pursuers than on getting out of the rain. She looked up when the finch returned, hoping the little bird was bringing good news. Landing on Liam's arm, the finch shook rain from her feathers and said, "Those men are coming up the last hill. They're going to catch up to you soon."

"That's all right," said Liam. "We're leaving the road now anyway."

Annie looked past him into the forest. "These woods look familiar."

"They should," Liam told her. "This is where we met Prince Cozwald."

"Then we must be close to Lizette and Grimsby's castle," said Annie.

"Which is exactly where we're going now," Liam said. "It should be right this way."

Annie was horrified. "No!" she exclaimed. "We can't go there!"

"Why not?" Liam said, looking surprised. "Is it because he's an ogre and tried to kill me the last time we met?"

"Of course not," said Annie. "It's just that I forgot to invite them to the wedding. I meant to, but it completely slipped my mind. I feel just awful!"

"You'll feel worse if we don't get out of this storm soon, or those men catch up with us. The ogre's castle is the only shelter that I know of around here."

Annie sighed. "Then I guess we have no choice, but I really don't like barging in on them!"

"At least this time we're not here to kill the ogre and rescue the princess," Liam said with a laugh.

"That's true," said Annie. "Although I still wouldn't call this a friendly visit, not with those men on our tails!"

Liam shook his head. "I don't like leading men like that to someone's home, but I don't see that we have any choice. I could probably handle them myself if I wasn't worried that I would risk leaving you unprotected.

I'm sure Grimsby and Lizette will understand. If we're lucky, those men will have enough good sense to stay away from an ogre's castle."

The mare following them whinnied again and Hunter screamed right back. "Great," Liam said. "We're trying to lose those men and this stallion keeps announcing where we are."

The storm grew stronger as they picked their way through the forest. Thunder rumbled and wind lashed the branches overhead, tossing leaves and bits of broken twigs to the forest floor. Boughs broke with a loud *crack!* crashing to the ground and making even the normally calm Otis skittery. Suddenly, out of the near-dark, the castle loomed overhead, looking as foreboding as it had the first time they'd been there.

Annie and Liam were trying to make their horses go closer when the little finch returned, landing on Liam's shoulder. If the bird chirped anything, Annie couldn't hear it over the sound of the wind and rain. "Did she say something?" Annie shouted to Liam.

"Those men are right behind us," he shouted back. "We have to get inside the castle."

"Do we have to climb the wall like last time?" Annie asked, looking up at the chiseled stone.

Thunder rumbled, sounding louder and closer. Liam nodded. "We will unless we can find another way in."

Annie followed Liam through the trees, looking for a door or window or any kind of opening. Anxious, she kept glancing back, expecting to see the men at any moment. When lightning flashed overhead, she thought she saw a horse and rider back among the trees, but then it was dark again and she was urging Otis on.

"What are we going to do with the horses?" Annie shouted at Liam. "We can't leave them in this storm. They'll either get hurt or run off."

"I haven't seen a shelter for them yet. We'll keep looking."

The wind was growing stronger, pushing against their backs. They were rounding the base of a tower when there was a loud crash and a door in the castle wall blew open, letting the rain pour in.

"This way!" Liam shouted, hopping down from his horse's back. "We'll have to leave the horses out here. I can hobble them and—"

Thunder boomed as lightning cracked the night sky overhead. Terrified, Liam's horse broke away and ran through the open door into the castle. Not wanting to be left behind, Otis followed, carrying Annie inside. She was sliding off Otis's back when Liam appeared. "I guess the horses decided for us," said Annie. "I don't have the heart to put them back outside now."

Annie helped Liam force the door shut. It was dark in the castle, with no lit torches and light only when lightning flashed. "The next time there's lightning, look for a torch on the wall or a candlestick or something I can light," said Liam.

"All right," Annie said as they waited in the dark. "You know, I've never ridden a horse into someone's home before. I have to say, though, that this is more like a very large house than a castle. There's no courtyard, no moat, no real defense . . ."

"It's an ogre's castle," said Liam. "Usually that would be defense enough. Ah, there we go!"

Lightning split the sky outside with an earthshaking boom, startling the horses and giving Annie and Liam the chance to look around. They were in a large hall with a fireplace at the other end. "I didn't see anything," said Annie. "Nothing on the walls, no furniture . . . It looks as if the place has been abandoned."

"I didn't see anything, either," said Liam. "Something isn't right."

"Here," Annie said, taking the wilted moonflower petals out of her knapsack. "We can use these." They were partly crushed and the edges were browner than before, but they still gave off enough light to see by.

"What happened to this place?" Liam asked as he looked around.

The hall looked as if it had been ransacked. There were no sconces on the walls, although Annie could see marks from smoke where candles or torches had burned. Rough stone remained where wood paneling had once covered surfaces, the floor was torn up in some places, and there were piles of rubble in others. The mantel and stone facing of the fireplace had been removed. All of the tapestries, furniture, and decorations were gone, leaving an empty shell behind.

"Lizette and Grimsby must have moved out," said Annie. "Then vandals broke in and did this. Now I don't feel so bad about bringing the horses inside."

"We need to find something to block this door," Liam said. "See, the latch is broken. That's why it blew open."

"We're not going to find anything here," said Annie. "And we can't stay where we are. Those men are going to be right behind us."

Liam nodded. "You're right. We'll leave the horses here. The men are after us, not the horses. Let me get you somewhere safe, then I'll come back down and deal with them."

They hurried from the hall with Annie carrying the petals to light their way. Entering a corridor, they saw a set of steps at the end. She recognized the staircase from their last visit. "We'll be safe up there," she said over her shoulder as she strode toward the stairs.

"Hurry," said Liam. "Those men are in the hall now."

Annie heard the thud of someone tripping in the dark and a grumbled curse even as another voice cried out, "Blast it! I've burned my fingers again on this stupid torch. Why didn't you bring one that works, Alfred?"

"At least I brought a torch, Fenley! We'd be stuck in the dark again if it had been up to you."

"There, I got it. Which way did they go?"

Annie and Liam ran up the stairs, one flight, then a second to a floor where the stairs ended at a corridor and closed doors. The men were behind them then, their feet pounding the steps.

Remembering their last visit, Annie turned to the door at the far end of the corridor. "We have to go this way," she told Liam.

"But that leads to—"

"I know," said Annie. "But if the magic is still working, the house can actually help us."

The last time they had entered the room, it had held a table and two chairs along with the remains of two meals. It was empty now, with nothing but dust and stale air to greet them. Annie glanced down the corridor as she closed the door behind them and could see the light of a torch wobbling as the men ran up the stairs. A head appeared at the landing and Annie was sure the man had spotted her.

"They'll be here in a moment," she told Liam. "Quick, this way!"

Annie had been the one to discover the secret staircase hidden behind a panel in the wall during their last visit. The door was covered with the same paneling that covered the walls, making it almost impossible to see. Because she knew where it was, she found the handle easily, opening the door without making a sound. They slipped through, closing it behind them, and started up the stairs just as the men threw open the door into the room and rushed inside. Annie paused on the stairs until she heard them fling open the door opposite the first and barge into the hallway beyond. She and Liam climbed a few more steps, then the men were back in the room, running through as if they had never seen it before. By the time Annie and Liam had neared the top of the secret staircase, the men had run through the room two more times.

"Wait a minute!" one of the men said. "Haven't we been here before?"

"What are you talking about, Alfred? We've never been near this castle before tonight."

"I don't mean the castle, I mean this room. I swear we keep going through it."

"How is that possible? We'll go out that door . . ."

"And come in this one. Stay here and watch me."

Annie heard the sound of running feet, then overheard one of the men left behind say, "Why are we listening to Alfred? While we stand here waiting, the prince and princess are getting away!"

"What do you want to do, Twitch? We could go after him, but he—"

"See!" Alfred said as he dashed into the room, panting.

"How did you come in that door? You just went out the other one!"

"It's like I said, we keep going through the same room. Someone put a spell on it."

"So where did the prince and princess go? Shouldn't they be running through the room, too?"

"They must have found another way out," said Alfred. "I don't see a trapdoor, so maybe there's a secret door in one of these walls. See if you can find one."

The men started tapping on the walls, working their way around the room.

Afraid of putting her weight on a squeaky step, Annie had stopped just below the top of the stairs while the men were in the room, but she and Liam no longer had time to wait. She started up the stairs again, gesturing for Liam to follow.

"I found it!" shouted one of the men, and the door at the bottom of the stairs flew open. "There they are!"

"Go!" Liam cried, urging Annie up the last few steps.

Unlike the floors below, this one looked just as it had before. Wooden benches lined the walls, one between each of the closed doors. Light from flaming torches wavered in a breeze that wafted through the windowless hallway. A tapestry's edge fluttered as if it were alive.

The moment Annie and Liam stepped into the hall-way, the air began to swirl around their feet, carrying black fur with it. Annie could hear the magic gathering, but she wasn't worried; she knew what was coming next and what she had to do about it. She and Liam ran down the corridor, heading to the far end. Although the fur followed Liam, it avoided her entirely.

"We've got 'em now!" shouted one of the men, who were nearly tripping over one another as they followed Annie and Liam.

Reaching the end of the hall with nowhere to go, Liam stepped in front of Annie, saying, "Stay behind me. I recognize those men and I've dealt with them before. I'll just . . . Drat this fur! I can't move!"

Annie glanced down. The fur had wrapped itself around Liam's feet and ankles and was working its way up his legs. No matter how much he strained to lift them, he couldn't budge his feet.

"Hold my hand," Annie told him. "And don't let go."

The moment Liam touched her, the fur fell away and skittered down the hallway toward the men, who were also unable to move. Some of the fur had already gathered around them, coating their boots. As more fur accumulated, it covered their legs, working its way up their bodies. Annie recognized them with a start. They were the men who had delivered the tiny spindle that had pricked Gwendolyn's finger and put everyone in the castle except Annie to sleep. They were the same men who had locked Annie in Rapunzel's tower. And now . . .

"Help me!" shouted one of the men, his eyes wild with fear as he beat at the thickening fur.

A door burst open and an ogre over seven feet tall thundered into the hallway. "What are you doing in my home?" he roared, waving a massive knobbed cudgel over his head.

"Grimsby!" cried Annie. "You're here after all!"

The ogre turned to glare at Annie. "Of course I'm here," he growled. "Did you come thinking I was away?"

"We came hoping you were home," said Liam. "But your door was open and your castle looked deserted."

"These men have been chasing us," Annie added. "We came to you for refuge."

"What's this?" Princess Lizette said, emerging from the same room. Clutching her robe at her throat with one hand, she rubbed the sleep from her eyes with the other. "Annie, Liam, what are you doing here? Is Cozwald here as well?"

Annie shook her head. "No, it's just us. These men have been following us since we reached Farley's Crossing."

"We didn't mean you any harm!" shouted the man called Alfred.

"Really?" said one of the others. "I thought we did. Have our plans changed again?"

"Quiet!" the ogre bellowed. His face was a mask of rage until he turned to Lizette. The anger fell away then, replaced with a look of such love that Annie had to squeeze Liam's hand. "What do you want me to do with them, my love?"

"Lock those men in the dungeon and throw away the key!" cried the princess. "Then come back upstairs and help me welcome our guests."

"No!" shouted Twitch. "Not an ogre's dungeon!"

"I told you we shouldn't have taken this job," said Alfred.

"Move along!" growled Grimsby.

"Wait!" Liam called. "I want them to answer a question first. Who hired you to come after us?"

"Don't answer him!" cried Fenley.

Grimsby took a step toward them, waving his cudgel. "You'll answer him or you'll answer to me!"

"I'd rather answer the prince," said Twitch. He turned his head, the only thing he could move, to look at Liam. "It was your brother, Clarence. He wanted us to get rid of you so you wouldn't interfere with his plans."

"What were his plans, exactly?"

"Take over Dorinocco, of course," he said as if he thought Liam was thickheaded.

"Then there's no longer any point to your mission," said Liam. "Clarence and my mother are both locked away now. I doubt very much that either will be getting out soon."

Fenley's mouth dropped open. "When did that happen?"

"Yesterday," said Annie. "King Montague is back on his throne again."

"Well, I'll be," Fenley muttered to himself.

"Next time I tell you that something is a bad idea, will you please listen to me?" Alfred asked as Grimsby herded them down the stairs. The job was made easier when the fur seemed to take over, making the men march in front of the ogre and go wherever he pointed. "We would have been better off if we'd taken that job my uncle Rudy offered us," Alfred continued. "He wanted us to ..."

Annie stopped listening as their voices faded away. It had been a long day and suddenly she was exhausted. She had to force herself to smile when Lizette beamed in her direction. "There," Lizette said. "Now we can talk. I want you to tell me everything, starting with why you're here."

Annie sighed. "I'd love to, but do you think we can change out of these wet clothes first?"

"Oh, I'm sorry! I might have some clothes that would fit you, Annie, although I'm not sure Grimsby would have anything for Liam. Right this way, and ... Oh, how sweet. You're holding hands."

"I'm trying to keep the fur off Liam," said Annie.

"Don't worry about the fur now. It's helping Grimsby. When he comes back upstairs he'll tell it to leave you alone and you'll be fine. But why do you think holding hands would help?"

"Because magic can't touch me, or anyone I touch," said Annie.

"Really? That's so interesting! I didn't know that about you. I see there's *a lot* you have to tell me."

"Is everything all right here?" asked Liam. "We thought vandals had ransacked your castle."

"Oh, that! We're having it redone. Grimsby had let it go, but he said I could do whatever I want to it. The choice was either redecorate the castle or go on a grand tour, but after the wedding I decided that I'd rather fix up the castle. We'll go on a grand tour later."

"You got married?" asked Annie.

"Just last week!" said Lizette, holding up her hand, where a diamond as big as a robin's egg sparkled on her finger. "I'm sorry we didn't invite you to the wedding, but it was a small affair with just a few hundred people."

They were still talking in the hallway when Grimsby came back up the stairs. "Did you know there were horses in the hall?"

"I'm so sorry!" said Annie. "I forgot to mention them. The horses are Liam's and mine. We didn't know where to put them and the storm was so bad . . ."

Grimsby shrugged. "No skin off my fangs. I put them in the stable, though. They were making a mess on the floor and the workmen won't like it."

"I was about to get Annie some dry clothes. Perhaps you can find something Liam can wear, at least until his own clothes are dry. You'll be spending the night, of course," Lizette said, turning to Annie. "You'll be our very first guests. We don't usually go to bed so early, but the workmen get here at daybreak and we like to be up and about before then. We're having them work on the top floor last, so there are two rooms all made up that will be perfect for you. Oh, dear, I suppose we should all get some sleep now. That's all right. We'll have a nice big breakfast in the morning and you can tell us everything then."

Good, thought Annie. Tomorrow would be soon enough.

CHAPTER 14

"Roar!"

Annie was out of bed, standing up, before she was even awake. The sound had been terrifying, and as she tottered on her feet, she looked around, half expecting to see the ceiling caving in or a dragon tearing down the walls. She was surprised to find that everything was just as she'd left it when she'd fallen asleep in the clean but shabby bedroom. The sound came again, just as loud and just as terrifying.

"Annie, are you all right?" Liam shouted, throwing open the door.

"I'm fine," she said as she hurried to join him. "What *was* that?"

"Good morning!" Lizette called out in a cheerful voice, appearing in the doorway of her own room. "I thought I'd let you sleep in while breakfast was cooking, but no one could sleep through that!"

"What made that sound?" Liam asked her.

"I'm sure it was just one of the workmen upset about something. It happens all the time. You get used to it eventually. Grimsby went downstairs to talk to them. He'll be joining us for breakfast, so if you'd like to get ready . . . ," Lizette said, giving Annie's borrowed nightgown a pointed glance.

"Give me five minutes," Annie said as she closed the door.

She turned around, surprised to see that her bed had been made and her own clothes were clean, dry, and draped across a chair. "That's odd," she murmured. She hadn't seen anyone, nor had she heard any magic.

It took her only minutes to get dressed. She was ready with her hair brushed and the nightgown folded neatly on the bed when the five minutes were up. The aroma of frying bacon and fresh-baked bread greeted her when she opened the door, making her mouth water. Lizette wasn't there, but a moment later Liam stepped out of the room across the hall.

"You *were* fast," said Liam. "Lizette said to go to the dining room at the bottom of the stairs when we were ready."

"But there was nothing in it," said Annie.

Liam shrugged. "We could sit on the floor for all I care, as long as they feed us."

"We need to get on the road as soon as we can," Annie told him as they started down the stairs.

Liam nodded. "We should reach the Garden of Happiness in just a few hours, then we can start back to your parents' castle."

"Why are you going to the Garden of Happiness?" Lizette asked as the door at the bottom of the stairs opened. "Sorry, I couldn't help but overhear you."

"We're looking for the fairy Moonbeam, and we were told she'd gone there to visit her friend," said Annie.

Lizette raised one eyebrow. "Why do you need Moonbeam?"

"It's a long story," Annie replied.

As she reached the bottom of the stairs, Annie was surprised to see that the table was back, along with four chairs and a sideboard. Grimsby was already seated at the table, drinking something cold and frothy. Platters of steaming bacon, biscuits, venison sausage, herbed pota-toes, and cooked mixed grains rested on the sideboard.

"Oh, my," said Annie. "Where did all this food come from? I mean, how could you cook it with your home so torn up?"

Lizette laughed, a loud shriek that reminded Annie of the first time they'd met. Annie and Liam had come with Cozwald, a prince who had thought Lizette needed rescuing, especially when they'd heard her shrieking and believed the ogre was killing her.

Annie and Liam both looked confused now, but Grimsby laughed with his bride, a gentle sound compared to the shrill noise she was making. When she was finally wiping tears from her eyes, she smiled at Annie and said, "I didn't cook any of this. Our servants did, just like they always do."

"What servants?" Liam asked, looking around.

"Our invisible servants, of course," said Lizette.

"Every wealthy ogre household has them," Grimsby explained.

"Someone did make my bed and wash my clothes," said Annie. "I didn't hear any magic, though."

Lizette gestured for Annie and Liam to help themselves from the sideboard. "You said last night that magic cannot touch you, so I assume you did your own hair. Otherwise the servants would have brushed your hair and helped you dress this morning."

"Doesn't that bother you?" asked Annie. "You'd never know when an invisible servant is in the room."

Lizette sighed. "It's just something else I had to get used to. Now, you never did tell me why you need Moonbeam. Is something wrong?"

Annie nodded. "Everything! Liam and I were supposed to get married a few days ago, but then one thing after another happened . . ."

While Annie and Liam piled their plates high with food and sat down to eat, they took turns telling Lizette and Grimsby about the day they were supposed to get married. They also told them about everything they'd gone through after leaving the castle.

"And now you want to see Moonbeam?" said Grimsby. "What are you going to ask her to do?"

Annie glanced at Liam. They hadn't really discussed what they would say to Moonbeam or what they needed from her. Annie knew they wanted her help, but she wasn't sure what form it should take. Knowing Moonbeam, it would be better to tell her something precise, rather than let her make it up as she went along.

Annie wanted Moonbeam to make the mischief stop, end King Dormander's siege, and send the evil wizard away. What she'd really like, however, was to have everything back the way it had been before their wedding was disrupted. Unfortunately, that kind of magic was probably more than even the most powerful fairy could handle.

"We're not sure what we're going to tell Moonbeam," Annie told Grimsby. "But we do have to decide soon."

"And we need to get going," Liam said, setting his tankard on the table. "We have a lot to do today."

"I was wondering, Lizette," Annie said as Liam got to his feet. "Would you and Grimsby like to come to our wedding? I know it's a little late to ask you, but—"

"We'd love to!" cried Lizette. "Wouldn't we, Grimsby?"

The ogre nodded, taking his bride's delicate hand in his big, rough one. "It will be the second wedding I've attended. Our wedding was the first."

"We're going to hold it as soon as we can after we have everything straightened out," said Annie. Liam pulled her chair back for her as she stood. "Thank you for your kind hospitality."

"And for locking up those men," said Liam. "If you wouldn't mind holding on to them for a few days, we should have everything settled."

"No problem," Grimsby replied. "I'll be right back, my love. I'm going to see our guests to the door."

"Annie, Liam, I'll see you soon!" called Lizette, waving good-bye as they started toward the stairs that led to the lower floors.

"Wait," Grimsby said when they reached the staircase. "I should go first. The workmen are down there and some of them aren't very happy right now."

Even from the top of the stairs they could hear hammering and the sound of heavy things being moved two floors below. Someone dropped something and yelped while someone else shouted orders. When the group reached the first floor and walked into the hall, Annie was glad that Grimsby had gone first. Three ogres who were bigger and nastier looking than Grimsby were carrying huge slabs of granite to the fireplace at the far end. Another ogre who was dragging an even heavier block stopped when he saw them, squinted his eyes, and growled.

"Now Lummox, these are friends of mine," said Grimsby. "No need to get worked up."

"Humans!" said the ogre. "They responsible for the mess I found this morning? Had to clean it up before I got started. No respect for other people's property, if you ask me. Not staying here, are they?"

"No, no, just passing through," Grimsby said as he hustled Annie and Liam to the door.

They walked around a crew of dwarves laying a new floor and a gnome carving woodwork. Every one of the workers looked at them with dislike. "They got Lummox mad, now we have to put up with him," one of them muttered.

"Sorry about the horses," Liam said once they were outside. "We didn't mean to make a mess."

"Or be disrespectful," said Annie.

"Don't listen to Lummox," Grimsby told them. "He's happiest when he has something to complain about. The servants had cleaned up the mess before he got here, but he said it wasn't clean enough. Ogres have a very refined sense of smell, you know. Even better than giants. You may have heard that giants can smell the blood inside your body. Some ogres can smell your bones. Here we go, the servants got your horses ready for you. Ogres don't ride, so I didn't have a stable before I married Lizette. I just had one built so she can keep some horses here. Good luck at the Garden of Happiness. I don't care for the place myself. Too cheerful for my taste, and way too many fairies!"

As Grimsby strode back into the castle, Annie and Liam turned to the horses. Their reins had been tied to a hitching post that hadn't been there the night before, and they both looked groomed and well fed. Otis nickered when he saw Annie, nuzzling her neck when she reached for his reins.

"That was an interesting visit," Annie said as Liam boosted her onto Otis's saddle. "I like Grimsby a lot more than I thought I would, although I didn't care for his workmen, especially Lummox."

"I guess ogres are like humans," Liam said as he untied his horse's reins. "Some are nicer than others. At least the weather is good today. We should reach the garden in a few hours."

"I just hope Moonbeam is there," said Annie. "We have no idea how my family is doing. I can't bear to be away from home much longer!"

⁓

The finch joined them before they had gone very far, trilling a wordless morning song. Annie liked it, but Liam looked annoyed and refused to let the bird sit on his shoulder while she was singing. When the finch finished her song, she hopped from Hunter's forelock back onto Liam's shoulder. "Where are we going today? Are you going to visit another ogre?"

"Actually, we're visiting a fairy," Annie told her. "She lives in a beautiful garden."

"I like gardens, especially the kind with seeds," the finch said, shifting from one foot to the other.

"You've already repaid me for letting you out of the ogre's cage," said Annie. "You don't need to watch over me any longer."

"But I haven't saved your life yet! Telling you things isn't enough. I'll be right back. I think I see a tasty worm!"

"So we have a new permanent companion?" Liam asked Annie as the finch flew to the ground.

Annie shrugged. "Or until she believes she's saved my life."

It was midafternoon when they reached the village closest to the Garden of Happiness. They passed the inn where they had eaten with Prince Andreas and continued on to the path that led to the garden belonging to the fairy Sweetness N Light. Lined with a wild profusion of flowers, the path was easy to find. Even in the shade of the forest, there were flowers growing hip high on both sides. Tempted by so many delicious plants, the horses struggled against their reins as Annie and Liam made them keep going.

It wasn't long before they spotted a brook running alongside the path. "Hello!" said the brook in a watery, wavery kind of voice. "How are you today? Have you ever . . . Wait, I remember you! Ooh! You are in trouble! Everyone is so mad at you. I can't believe you're here."

"Why are we in trouble?" asked Annie. "What have we done to make them mad?"

"If you don't know, I'm not going to tell you," said the brook. "But I will tell everyone that you're here. There, I just did. They're getting worked up now! Ooh, Dandelion's face is so red, I think she's going to pop! And Lupine is clenching her fists. And Snapdragon is—"

"That's enough," said Liam. "We don't need a complete rundown of how mad everyone is."

"Is Sweetness N Light here?" asked Annie. "Does she have a guest named Moonbeam?"

The brook gasped. "How did you know? Have you been spying on us? I wouldn't put it past someone as low and sneaky and—"

"What did we do? Why are you saying these things?" Annie asked.

"I don't know," said the brook. "You should ask Sweetness N Light. She's mad at you, too."

"Look, there they are!" cried a fairy as a group of them flew into the woods. "You have a lot of nerve coming here, Princess!"

"Why? What did we do?" Annie asked them.

"Don't play stupid with us! We know you know what you did. You did it on purpose, too, so don't fib and say you didn't."

"But I... Ow! That hurt!" One of the fairies had thrown a berry at her, hitting her right between the eyes.

Suddenly the air was filled with flying berries as the fairies pelted Annie and Liam. Liam shouted and swatted at the fairies, while Annie wrapped her arms around her head and ducked. Fortunately, Otis kept walking, carrying them down the path to the open meadow. Liam chased most of the fairies off, so Annie was able to dismount without getting hit. The gelding started cropping flowers before Annie had dismounted, and didn't seem to care when she tied his reins to a tree branch.

"Where will we find Sweetness N Light?" Annie asked the brook.

"At the waterfall," said the brook even as a chorus of fairies sang out, "Don't tell them anything!"

Annie and Liam knew the way to the waterfall, but it wasn't as easy to reach as it had been the last time. Although the white-stone path was empty of flowers, it was filled with fairies no bigger than Annie's little finger, getting in their way while insulting them by calling out, "Stinky Breath," "Werewolf Butt," "Moldy Pants," and even more awful names.

Liam acted as if they weren't there, putting his feet down wherever he wanted to, so that they had to dart out of the way or risk getting squashed. Annie was more careful, however, trying to place her feet to avoid stepping on the fairies who were taunting her. The fairies soon saw what she was doing and began to gather in front of her so she had no place to step.

Liam glanced back when he realized that she wasn't with him. "Just keep walking or they'll never let you past."

Still not wanting to hurt them, Annie began to shuffle forward, trying to push them out of her way. That seemed to make them angrier, however, and they attacked her. While some snagged her feet to trip her, others tried to push her into the brook.

"Oh, no, you don't!" the brook cried when Annie staggered and almost fell into the water. "I don't want her near me."

"I'll save you, Princess!" the finch chirped, seeming to appear out of nowhere. Fluttering her wings, the finch flew in the faces of the fairies that were shoving at Annie, chirping madly all the while. The fairies backed off, and Annie was able to regain her balance.

The fairies were about to attack her again when Liam turned around. Scowling, he strode to her side and scooped her up, cradling her in his arms as he headed for the waterfall. Although the fairies clustered around Liam and called out names, they kept their distance and didn't try to trip him.

Annie and Liam didn't have to go far before they reached the top of the waterfall. Passing the underbrush, they saw three full-size people sitting beside the pool at the base of the falls. All three were sipping from tulip cups and eating peeled grapes. While the two fairy women laughed and chatted, the third person, a short, pudgy, balding man, looked bored, as if he'd rather be anywhere but there.

At the approach of the prince and princess, the man looked up. He was smiling when he nudged his wife and said, "Look who's here!"

Moonbeam's mouth spread wide in a huge smile when she saw them. "My two most favorite people!" she cried. "Without you, I never would have met my beloved Selbert!" Scooting to the side, she patted the ground beside her. "Come join us!"

The moment she laid her eyes on them, Sweetness N Light began to scowl. It wasn't an ordinary scowl, but a fearsome scowl that would have looked more fitting on the face of Terobella, the evilest witch in all the kingdoms, if she hadn't already been turned into snail slime.

"What are you doing here?" Sweetness N Light asked as if the words tasted bad. "You're not welcome in my garden, especially after what you've done!"

"What are you talking about?" asked Annie.

Sweetness N Light's scowl deepened. Raising her hand high in the air, she made an intricate gesture while calling out, "Come to me, my fairy friends. I have work for you to do! Take these two and—"

"I mean it," said Annie. "What are you talking about? Your fairies said I had done something, but they wouldn't tell me what it is."

"Don't play stupid with me!" Sweetness N Light snarled.

Annie had had enough. After everything she had gone through, she didn't need or deserve the disdain of the fairies as well. Suddenly, she lost her temper, something she so rarely did that even Liam looked at her in surprise. "I am not playing anything," she shouted. "I invite you to my wedding and you don't even bother to reply, let alone show up. Then someone uses magic to ruin my wedding, and a king I've never even heard of lays siege to the castle and there's a storm and everything is flooded and I have to go look for Moonbeam! Then every fairy in Treecrest treats me like I'm some horrible monster! No, I don't know what I did to deserve this, but I'm tired of worrying about everyone else and thinking about their feelings when it was supposed to be my wedding day. Instead of being the person to help everyone, I'm the one who people should help for a change! Isn't it enough that all these awful things happened, without you tormenting me as well?"

By the time Annie finished, she was quivering with rage, but when she looked around at all their astonished faces, she was suddenly too tired and too overcome to care about anything. Putting her hands over her face, she let her legs fold under her and she sat down for a good hard cry.

"You invited us?" asked Sweetness N Light, turning from Annie to Liam.

Liam nodded. "We sent out the invitations weeks ago. Your helper Squidge delivered them personally," he said to Moonbeam.

"But we never got them," said Sweetness N Light.

"No, we didn't," said all the little fairies.

Moonbeam looked perplexed. "Squidge was helping you? Why would he do that?"

"He said you were away so you didn't need him until you returned. He said he wanted to repay us for bringing you and Selbert together."

"That's odd," said Moonbeam. "He was very upset that I married Selbert. When I told him how we met, he could only say unkind things about you. I'll have to ask him about it when I see him next."

Annie wiped the tears from her eyes. "You're not going to see him again. I'm so sorry."

Moonbeam frowned. "Something happened to Squidge?"

"He'd been trying so hard to be helpful and he went up on the battlements with us," Annie told her. "There was a strong wind because of the storm and it carried him off. I'll never forget the way he screamed."

"Is *that* all?" Moonbeam said, looking relieved. "Then he's fine. He's a weather sprite; controlling the weather is second nature to him. I made him my assistant because he's so good at calling up the rain and watering my moonflowers."

"You mean he can control the wind?" asked Liam.

Moonbeam nodded. "Sometimes he does it for fun."

"Then he wasn't in danger? He didn't die or get hurt or anything awful?" asked Annie.

"Not likely," Moonbeam said. "He probably called the wind himself."

"Let me get this straight," said Liam. "Squidge tricked us when he pretended to be carried off. And if he really didn't like us, he probably tricked us when he pretended to help. He never did deliver the invitations, but just pretended to do it. Am I right?"

Moonbeam's frown was back. "It sounds like it. Why, that little scoundrel! I know that sprites like to make mischief, but he's never given me a bit of trouble."

"If he could control the weather," said Liam, "could he have called up the storm?"

"You said it flooded the castle? Then I doubt it. He could make it rain, and he could call up the wind, but a really big storm would have required the touch of a witch or powerful fairy."

Sweetness N Light rubbed her cheek and looked everywhere but at Annie or Liam. "Uh, about that. The storm was actually my doing. If it flooded things, well, I might have gotten a little carried away, but we were so angry when we thought you hadn't invited us!"

"But what about everything else? My dress getting ruined and the moving rashes and the animals and, well . . . everything?" asked Annie.

"None of the fairies or witches in the kingdom received invitations," said Sweetness N Light. "That's a lot of beings with magic who were angry at you."

"Can you please talk to them? Can you make them stop now?" Annie asked.

"We'll do more than that," said Sweetness N Light. "We'll get them to help us set things right. We were all mad at you when we shouldn't have been and we took it out on you. I don't often admit to being wrong, but we all were in this case, and it's up to us to make it up to you. Just tell us what you need us to do and we'll do it."

"It's a long list," warned Liam.

"And I know a lot of fairies," Sweetness N Light replied.

CHAPTER 15

ANNIE AND LIAM WATCHED as an iridescent, vibrantly colored cloud formed above the waterfall and headed north. The second round of tiny fairies had been sent to spread the word that all the fairies and witches in the kingdom had been invited to the wedding. Now nearly half of the flower fairies that lived in the Garden of Happiness were seeking friends and relatives who lived in other parts of the kingdom, informing them that they had all made a big mistake and needed to make up for it. A separate group had gone to tell the witches, a job they did with reluctance.

"Don't worry," Sweetness N Light told Annie. "I'll see that everyone reverses their spells and cleans up the mess they made. I'm going to the castle myself to repair any damage that my storm caused."

"Thank you," said Annie. "That will help a lot. However, that still leaves King Dormander. I'd never even heard his name before he showed up in Treecrest, but I've been thinking and I might have an idea who he is. There's someone I need to talk to at the castle. I have to get back as soon as I can."

"I could whisk you there with my magic," Moonbeam said, holding up her wand.

Annie shook her head. "Magic doesn't work on me, remember? The rest of you could get there that way, but I need to use a more conventional means of travel. If I ride Otis, I should be there in a few hours."

"I assume Otis is a horse," said Sweetness N Light. "And that your prince will go with you."

"Of course," Liam replied.

"Then we'll go on ahead," said Moonbeam. "We have a lot to do and I want to get started."

"I don't suppose you could help us with King Dormander," said Liam.

"We can't," Sweetness N Light told him. "Other than helping individuals, fairies don't get involved in human matters, and we avoid wars in particular. We'll clean up the mess we made, but the rest is up to you."

Knowing that the fairies were on their way to the castle made Annie even more eager to go home. She and Liam left the garden already wondering how they were going to deal with King Dormander.

As they started on the road that led north to the castle, Liam turned to Annie, saying, "You said you had to talk to someone in the castle. Who do you mean?"

"A friend of mine," said Annie. "We've been calling her Lilah, but that isn't her real name. She has a lot of secrets and I'm hoping one of them can help us."

"Isn't that the girl who used to wear those ratty furs?"

Annie laughed. "They were mice and squirrel, actually, but yes, that's her. I hope everyone at home is all right. We've been gone way too long and who knows what King Dormander has done. I've been so worried about them and now that we're going home, I'm afraid of what we'll find."

"They'll be all right," said Liam. "I'm sure of it. Your father is a wise man, and your uncle is there, and Beldegard and Maitland and—"

"I know, they're all strong men who will make sure everyone is well, but I won't stop worrying until I see them all again."

"What do you think your family will do when the fairies and witches show up?"

"They'll be fine as long as Moonbeam gets there first to explain it all," Annie said. "My parents are hoping to see her, but they might not know what to do if the others arrive before her."

"I've been thinking," Liam began. "If the fairies are able to set things straight, and we get King Dormander to leave, I think we should get married as soon as possible."

Annie smiled at him. "I've been thinking the same thing! I know I got upset this morning when we were with the fairies, but honestly, this time I don't care what my gown looks like or if my attendants have purple spots and green stripes. I want to marry you no matter what as soon as possible."

"There's something else," Liam told her. "I know we had been planning to go on a grand tour, but we've been traveling a lot lately. Are you tired of traveling? Because if you are, we can stay home now and go in a few years."

"I want to go now! I would like to visit somewhere new, though. Do you have any place in mind?"

"No, but I'm sure we can come up with something. Why don't we both think about it and talk again later."

"All right, but I want it to be somewhere exotic and very different from Treecrest or Dorinocco."

"Sounds ideal," Liam said, giving her a warm smile.

They talked of the wedding then and how they would make do with what they had, but as they drew closer to the castle, their conversation waned as Annie became lost in thought and Liam became ever more wary. Soon after that, Liam made them leave the road and wend their way through the trees. Even without the road to guide them, he knew which way to go. Once they reached the part of the forest that Annie recognized, she knew how close they had come.

They were beside a small stream, in the deep shade of the forest, when Liam reined his horse in. "We'll leave the horses here. We can't take them any closer without the risk that they'll give us away. Don't worry," he said when he saw Annie's face. "We'll come back for them when it's over."

Instead of tying the horses to a branch, he hobbled them so they couldn't wander far. "We have to be very quiet now," he told Annie. "King Dormander could have men anywhere in these woods."

"There's a tunnel into the castle. It's right over there," Annie whispered, pointing deeper into the woods. "Wait! I hear magic. It's just up ahead. Slow down. I don't want to walk into it blindly. We should—"

Liam pulled Annie to a halt and put his finger to his lips. "Listen!" he breathed.

Someone was coming through the woods, not making any effort to be quiet. The sounds were faint, but definitely headed their way.

"In here," Liam said, moving toward a clump of ancient rhododendrons whose leaves promised some cover.

Annie and Liam worked their way between the bushes, crouching low to the ground. It wasn't long before a group of soldiers rode past close enough that Annie could hear the creaking of leather. She held her breath and willed them not to look her way. The cover that the shrubs provided was spotty at best, and she was afraid that one of the men might be able to see the two figures hiding behind the leaves.

The men had scarcely gone by when a doe walked past, heading in the direction of the castle. Annie squeezed Liam's hand and pointed. Liam nodded, and they watched in silence as the doe approached a gap between the trees. The animal had just set her foot on a pile of dead leaves when fire flared up under her hooves. Startled, the animal reared, nearly falling over. Scrambling backward, she turned and ran, crashing through the forest.

Annie had heard the magic grow louder just before the fire flared. The moment the deer moved away, the sound became faint again. When nothing else happened, Annie slipped out of the cover of the bushes and hurried to the place where she'd seen the fire. Liam was at her side when she bent down to inspect the ground. There were reddish patches that seemed to move, and they . . .

"They're fire ants. There's a line of them going off in both directions. Look, they're already moving away from me. I bet the line forms a loop around the castle, starting at the river's edge on both sides. Anyone who steps on the ants will make them burst into flame."

"Anyone but you, that is," said Liam.

"And you, if you hold my hand. Keep your eyes open. I doubt this is the only barrier the wizard set."

Annie took Liam's hand and together they walked across the line of ants. It was more than two yards wide and extended as far as she could see. Each time Annie or Liam took a step, the ants skittered away, maintaining a clear space around them. It took only a few steps to get to the other side, and when they stopped to look back, they could see the ants filling in the spots they had vacated.

"That wasn't so bad," Liam said as they started to walk again.

But Annie wasn't really listening. She had heard something, but it was too faint to tell if it was magic or someone humming a tune. Another step and it was louder. Two more and she knew for sure. "There's more magic right in front of us," she told Liam. "I think it's that patch of grass. See, there's another one, and another. They're spaced so if you miss one, you'll step on the next."

Although Annie was anxious to get back into the castle to see her family, she knew better than to rush into unknown magic. The sound she heard was faint, but frantic.

"What does it do?" Liam asked, bending down for a closer look.

"I don't know. I . . . What are you doing? Don't go that close!"

Liam had picked up a twig and was about to poke the grass with it. Hearing Annie, he shrugged and tossed the stick so that it landed on the grass. The blades of grass twitched, and suddenly they were whacking at the twig like a chef slicing a carrot, chopping it ever smaller and finer. Within moments the twig was reduced to a sawdust outline of itself. Annie watched as the grass shivered and the sawdust fell to the ground between the blades. When the grass moved back in place, the sawdust was hidden from view.

"Wow! Did you see that?" said Liam. "I pity the poor creature that steps on that grass."

"Hold on tight," Annie said, taking his hand again. "We don't have far to go."

Gripping Liam's hand so hard her knuckles were white, Annie stepped to the edge of the grass and looked down. The blades closest to the edge curled away from her feet and lay flat to the ground as if a stream of water were passing over them.

"Now!" she said, and they ran across the patch together, laughing in relief when they reached the other side.

"There may be more barriers," said Annie, "but the opening to the tunnel is in those rocks right there. Let me go first to make sure that there's no new magic around them or that the magic inside hasn't changed since I was here last."

Letting go of Liam's hand, she walked slowly toward the rocks, straining her ears for any little sound. When she didn't hear anything unexpected, she turned and gestured to Liam.

"At least this tunnel is dry, unlike the last one," Liam said as he peered inside.

"Thank goodness," Annie replied.

Holding the petals in front of her, she began to walk as fast as she could. Roots dangled from the ceiling, brushing their hair and making her jump the first time she felt one. She ducked then, trying to avoid the roots and remember if they had hung so low the last time she had gone this way. When she finally reached the bottom of the stairs, she didn't pause, but started up them at a near run. She was about to see her family and find out if they were all right.

Reaching the top of the stairs, Annie searched for the latch that held the secret door closed. It took her a moment to open it and push aside the tapestry that hid the door from curious eyes. There was a rustling sound in the chamber on the other side of the tapestry, and when she peeked out from behind it, she gasped. The room seemed to be full of soldiers and all of them were pointing their swords at her. At first she thought that King Dormander had taken over the castle, but then she recognized the men and her father stepped forward.

"Annie, my dear! You're back!" he said as the soldiers lowered their swords. "We heard you on the stairs and thought one of Dormander's men had found the tunnel. We didn't block this one or the one you used to get out so you could have a way back in. You can't know how relieved I am that you're here. Ah, Liam, it's good to see you, my boy. How was your trip? No need to tell me that it was a success. Moonbeam arrived a few hours ago and told us that you had sent her. Come and sit down. I want to hear about everything."

"I'm sorry, Father, but I have to go talk to someone first. It's urgent. I may know of a way to end the siege. Liam can stay and answer all of your questions. Do you mind, Liam?"

"Not at all," he said, and gave her a kiss on the cheek.

Annie wasn't sure where she would find Lilah, but she had a few ideas. She would check the kitchen first, and then the garden, and perhaps the . . . The moment she stepped out of her father's meeting chamber, she was surrounded. Everyone wanted to talk to her and they all had questions to ask. She put them off, one after another, saying that she would answer their questions soon. A crowd trailed behind her as she walked, but she refused to stop and talk to anyone. Time and again she explained that she had something important to do and that there would be plenty of time to talk later.

She was on her way through the great hall when Gwendolyn waylaid her, standing directly in her path and moving in front of her every time she tried to go past. The crowd that had been following Annie gathered around them, their numbers swelling as people learned that she was there.

"You're going to talk to me and you're not getting out of it," her sister told her. "Is anyone coming to help us—aside from the fairies, I mean?"

"No one else is coming," said Annie. "The fairies have already done a lot, from what I can see."

As she'd walked through the corridors, people had told her that her bridesmaids no longer had rashes, and that the fairies had fixed the roofs and floors, replaced the stones in the damaged walls, and rid the castle of all the animals that weren't supposed to be there. She had seen evidence of some of this and was pleased that they had been able to accomplish so much in so little time.

"But Father says they refuse to do anything about the wizard!" said Gwendolyn. "Couldn't you have found someone who would actually help us?"

Annie glanced at the avid faces surrounding her. Instead of thinking of them as a hindrance, perhaps she could enlist their help. "There is someone who might be able to help, but she's already here. I was on my way to find her. Does anyone know where Lilah is now?"

"Who is Lilah?" people asked one another.

"Doesn't she work in the kitchen?" a voice piped up.

"I think I saw her by the dovecote," said another.

"You stay here. We'll go find her!" called a third, and half the people in the crowd ran off in different directions.

"Good," said Gwendolyn. "Now you can talk to me. Where have you been exactly, and what have you been doing?"

"I've been all over, looking for Moonbeam. I'm sure Father told you that," Annie said.

"Yes, but you were gone for days! Did it really take that long to find one fairy?"

Annie didn't think she should tell her sister everything before she talked to the king, but once Gwendolyn got an idea in her head, it was hard to distract her. However, if there was one thing that her sister liked more than getting people to tell her things, it was being the center of attention.

"She wasn't easy to find," Annie replied. "Now it's your turn. What have you been doing while I was away? Has King Dormander's wizard tried any more magic?"

"As a matter of fact," Gwendolyn began, "the other morning he sent pigeons to spy on us, but it was my idea to—"

"We found her! She was in the buttery," a kitchen maid said, dragging a reluctant-looking Lilah by the hand.

"What do you want?" Lilah asked, shaking off the girl's grip.

"Just to talk to you," said Annie. Hearing the shuffle of feet, she looked around to see that everyone had moved closer to listen. "In private," she added, and led Lilah from the hall.

Grumbles of disappointment followed them as Annie took Lilah to a small room off the main corridor and shut the door.

"There's something you need to tell me," Annie said, turning to her friend. "Is King Dormander your father?"

Lilah looked away, letting her long hair cover her face. She nodded, an almost imperceptible movement that spoke volumes. "I should have told you sooner, but

187

I couldn't at first, and then when I wanted to, you were gone."

"Why couldn't you tell me when he first arrived? Are you that afraid of him?"

"Not of him. Of his wizard. He's the man my father wants me to marry. If you'd seen him doing the things I've seen, you'd know why I can't marry him."

"If he's so awful, why does your father want you to marry him?"

"Because the man acts normal when my father is around. Father has no clue what his wizard is really like. I've seen him hurt animals for fun, and kick and slap his servants. He lies, swearing that he's telling the truth even when the evidence is right in front of you. Sometimes he uses his magic to hurt people, which he thinks is funny. The man says he loves me, but that's not possible. The only person he loves is himself. I wanted to tell my father what the man was really like, but every time I tried, the wizard would show up."

"Then there is only one thing we can do. We'll have to *show* your father what the wizard is really like. You can't hide here forever, Lilah. Uh, what is your real name?"

"Mertice. It was my father's mother's name."

"Then come with me, Mertice. We're going to dress you in clothes worthy of a princess who is going to confront her father with the truth."

CHAPTER 16

"I ALREADY TOLD you that I can't get involved in human matters, especially not a war," Moonbeam told Annie and Liam.

"But you did say that you help individuals, and that's what we're asking you to do," said Annie. "Mertice's father wants her to marry an awful man. He just doesn't know how awful he is. We need your help to show him the truth."

"I don't know . . . ," said Moonbeam.

"What if someone had forced you to marry a man you couldn't stand?" Annie asked her. "Then you would never know the happiness you've had with Selbert, and you'd be miserable for the rest of your life. Please help us, Moonbeam? The only way we're going to end the siege is if Mertice goes back to her father, but we can't make her go back knowing that she'll end up married to a horrible person."

"I suppose…"

"Do you have a wedding present for us?" Liam asked.

"Why, no," said Moonbeam. "I hadn't thought about it yet."

"Then this could be your gift to us. Help Mertice and you don't have to give us anything else."

"That's a wonderful idea!" Annie said, beaming at Liam.

Moonbeam sighed. "Oh, all right. If it means that much to you! When do you want to go?"

"Right now!" Annie said. She was so pleased that she couldn't help herself and gave the fairy a hug.

The fairy looked surprised. "Well!" she exclaimed, and patted Annie's shoulder as if she didn't know what else to do.

"Is Mertice ready yet?" asked Liam.

Annie nodded. "She should be waiting in the great hall by now."

No one followed them when they stepped out of the room where they'd been talking. Annie had already noticed that most of the people in the castle kept their distance from the fairies and were particularly intimidated by Moonbeam and Sweetness N Light. Walking down the corridor was easier now and they soon reached the great hall. They found Mertice there, dressed in a deep blue gown with embroidery at the neck and wrists. It was one of Ella's gowns, since she was the only princess as tall as Mertice. She stood when she saw them, smoothing the soft fabric over her hips.

"You look very nice," said Annie.

"It feels strange to wear good clothes again," Mertice replied. "It's been so long."

"It didn't need to be," Annie said.

Mertice gave her a rueful smile. "I know. You've been very kind."

"Tell me about this man your father wants you to marry," Moonbeam said to Mertice.

While the princess talked to the fairy, Liam took Annie aside. "Don't you think we should tell your father what we're doing?"

"Not at all. He wouldn't let us do it if we did."

"Which tunnel do you want to use?" Liam asked.

"Neither," said Annie. "We'll have the south drawbridge lowered and go out the gate. King Dormander is getting exactly what he asked for—his daughter back. There's no need to hide from him now."

"Then I'll have some horses brought around," said Liam. "And a guard to carry a white flag. No need to risk Dormander's archers taking potshots at us by mistake."

"I don't ride horses," Moonbeam announced as she and Mertice joined them. "Never have, never will."

"Then we'll walk," said Annie. "We need to go out together."

They had to wait a few minutes while a guard found a white flag, but then they were out the door, watching the drawbridge lower. Annie noticed that a change seemed to be coming over Mertice. Instead of the hunched back and furtive look she'd assumed as Lilah, her back became straight, she held her head high, and her gaze was direct. She looked regal now, and no one could doubt that she was a princess.

As the drawbridge lowered enough that Annie could see over the top, she spotted King Dormander's soldiers gathered, ready to fight anyone who emerged from the castle.

"I'll go first," said Mertice. "They need to see that I'm here."

With the flag-carrying guard beside her, Mertice crossed the drawbridge while Annie, Liam, and Moonbeam followed close behind. A shout went up when they saw Mertice, and some officers rode out to greet her. Other soldiers moved as if to separate the princess from the rest of her party, but she refused to let anyone get between them.

"Stay back!" she called.

They bowed low and kept their distance as they shepherded the little party through the ranks to the king's tent. When Annie saw the angry looks they were giving her and Liam, she moved a little closer to her prince.

Mertice and her friends waited outside the tent until the curtain-door opened and a guard stepped out. "The king is anxious to see you, Your Highness, but these people must remain outside."

"Then I will remain outside as well," Mertice told him.

The man looked taken aback. "Uh, just a minute," he replied, and disappeared into the tent.

"Have you seen the looks they're giving us?" said Moonbeam. "No one has ever looked at me with such hatred before. It's rather disconcerting."

"They seem to think we've done something, but I can't imagine what," Annie told her.

"You may all enter," the guard said when he finally came back to hold the curtain-door open.

Mertice hooked one of her arms through Annie's and the other through Liam's, making sure that they would go in together. Annie didn't know what to expect when they entered the tent. Glancing back at Moonbeam, she saw that the fairy was following close behind, examining everything with great interest. Dressed in ordinary clothes rather than her normally sparkling garments, she looked like a kindly grandmother who baked tarts for visitors to her cottage and not at all like a powerful fairy.

The tent was large and yellow with a high pointed roof. The light passing through the fabric walls of the tent was bright and sunny, giving the space an almost golden glow. Colorful rugs covered the bare earth, and wooden benches were placed along the walls. Unlit lanterns hung from the ceiling, and a large banner depicting a shark chasing a dragon hung behind a tall chair in the middle of the tent.

The king was seated in the chair, with courtiers and armed guards flanking him on either side. A brown dog with a white muzzle snored at his feet. Mertice's father was a large man with black hair flecked with white, and a beard more white than black. His eyes looked troubled until he spied his daughter. They brightened then as if someone had lit a candle inside him.

"My beautiful girl!" he cried, getting to his feet. "It really is you. How are you? Have they hurt you?"

"Your Majesty," Mertice said, sounding formal, although her expression was warm. Freeing her arms from Annie's and Liam's, she curtsied to the king, but made no attempt to go any closer. Instead she glanced at the bald-headed man standing beside the king and her expression changed to one of dislike.

Annie studied the man, certain that he must be the wizard. He wore a dark gray robe with long, dangling sleeves that nearly reached the ground. His scalp was bare and so smooth that it almost looked as if it had been polished. Tufts of hair sprouted from his ears and nose, while bushy eyebrows overshadowed small eyes set close together. Annie thought he looked sly when he smiled at the princess.

"Come here, my dear girl, and let me look at you," said the king. "I'm glad these people finally came to their senses and allowed you to leave."

"These are my friends, Father," Mertice told him. "They brought me to see you not because of your siege, but because they just learned that I am your daughter. Allow me to introduce them to you. This is Princess Annabelle, Prince Liam, and . . ." She turned to Moonbeam and bit her lip. "I'm sorry. I don't believe I know your name."

The wizard leaned toward the king and whispered in his ear.

"Speak up, Rotan," said Mertice. "Whispering like that is rude. Tell us all what you told my father."

"I said," the wizard said, sneering, "that you are under their influence. They are controlling you now as much as they did when you were locked in their castle."

"They are not controlling me and they never held me prisoner! They gave me refuge when I needed it and treated me well."

"They didn't kidnap you?" asked the king.

"No one kidnapped me, Father. I left home of my own volition. I overheard you promise Rotan that I would marry him and that is something I will never do. I disguised myself and crossed the sea so I would not have to marry that man."

The king frowned. "You would disobey me in this? But you have always been such an obedient daughter."

"And you have always been a reasonable father, until you promised me to Rotan. He isn't what you think he is. He has never shown you what he is really like."

"I admit that he is many years older than you, and I suppose he is not as handsome as some, but he will take care of you after I am gone. I worry that you will be left all alone after I die."

"That won't be for many years, Father! If you give me a chance, I'm sure I can find a more suitable husband than Rotan."

Annie noticed that the wizard was glowering at Mertice during her conversation with the king. He kept opening and closing his mouth as if he were struggling not to interrupt, but his expression was getting angrier. Finally he could no longer control himself and he blurted out, "It's all lies, Your Majesty. I am just as you know me to be, a good honest man who has nothing but the well-being of you and your daughter at heart."

"So you're calling the princess a liar?" asked Annie as she took a step forward.

The wizard narrowed his already small eyes at her. "I would never do that! I'm saying that you have used some sort of magic to control her and the words she speaks."

"I don't use magic," said Annie.

"Really?" said the wizard. "Then why can I sense a magical presence? Let's check the truth of your words, shall we?"

His hands had been hidden inside his long sleeves, but he raised one now so that the sleeve fell back, exposing his hand and the slender wand it was clutching. Annie reached for Liam, grabbing his wrist as the wizard pointed his wand. In the next instant, the finch flew from where she had been resting on top of the banner and fluttered in the wizard's face, beating him with her wings and trying to peck him. Cursing, the wizard swatted her aside, knocking her to the ground at Moonbeam's feet.

Annie gasped and was about to reach for the finch when Liam called out, "Annie!"

She looked up in time to see the wizard point his wand at the chain holding up one of the lanterns. The loose end of the chain grew longer until it reached the ground, then longer still, sliding across the carpet to where Annie and Liam stood.

When Liam reached for his sword, Annie shook her head and whispered, "Remember the ants." Even though she was sure the chain wouldn't touch her, Annie held her breath while it reared back as if it were a snake about to strike, then whipped at her, only to stop in midair. It shivered so hard that the lantern attached to the other end rattled as it swung wildly on the ceiling of the tent. The chain backed off, then turned to Liam. Once again it moved as if to strike, only to be turned aside.

With an exasperated sigh, the wizard flicked his wrist and the chain fell in a heap on the carpet, inanimate once again. He gave Annie a speculative look and pointed his wand at the dog asleep at the king's feet. A tiny wave of the wand and the dog turned into a huge black wolf. The beast jumped to its paws and turned toward Annie and Liam, growling. Its eyes seemed to glow as it stalked them. And then it was hurling itself at Annie, its lips pulled back in a fearsome snarl.

Liam's sword snicked out of its sheath, but the wolf bounded to Annie's other side, coming at her so that Mertice and Annie herself blocked Liam's blow. The wolf was almost on her when Annie threw up her hand as if in defense. At her touch, the wolf turned back into the old dog and collapsed, groaning, its sides heaving.

"Rex!" Mertice cried, dashing to the dog and kneeling down beside it.

"You see!" shouted the wizard. "The girl has magic just as I said!"

"What did you do to my dog?" the king said, scowling at the wizard.

"It's just a dog, Your Majesty. You can always get another. I've proven that the girl is a witch."

"But I'm not," said Annie. "You've just proven that you don't like animals and that your magic doesn't work on me." Turning to Moonbeam, she asked in a soft voice, "Can you do something about him before he seriously hurts someone?"

"It would be my pleasure," the fairy said with a grim smile. Raising her own wand, she circled it overhead. The air seemed to crackle around them, the light grew almost unbearably bright, and suddenly Annie, Liam, Mertice, King Dormander, and the wizard were standing with the fairy in a meadow with no one else around.

The wizard looked more stunned than anyone else.

"You might want to get your father out of the way," Annie told Mertice.

The princess nodded and ran to her father, whose chair had also come to the meadow. Helping him to his feet, she hustled him away from any errant magic.

The wizard turned to Annie. "You've proven my point for me. Only someone with great magical powers could have done this. And anyone with such powers could easily control the mind of a princess."

"I didn't do it," said Annie.

"I did," Moonbeam declared.

"You're the witch!" exclaimed the wizard.

"Not quite," Moonbeam said with a laugh.

The wizard raised his wand and aimed it at Moonbeam, saying, "I know how to deal with you!" He wore a satisfied smile as a light shot from the tip of his wand, but instead of striking Moonbeam, it faded away before it could reach her. Muttering to himself, the wizard tried again, but the second attempt was no more successful than the first.

"Now it's my turn," said the fairy. With a twitch of her wand, the wizard's long sleeves wrapped them-selves around him, holding his hands and arms to his sides and covering his mouth so that he couldn't speak. Still pointing the wand at him, Moonbeam announced in a loud, clear voice,

> *The truth is like a beacon*
> *Shining in the night.*
> *It cuts through all the murkiness*
> *That can impede one's sight.*
> *Ensure this man will now speak*
> *Only what is true.*
> *So all may know what he has done*
> *And hear his point of view.*

"There," she said, glancing at Annie. "That ought to do it. Although I must say, I'm surprised that he didn't recognize me for what I am." Walking up to the still-bound man, she leaned toward him and shouted in his face, "I'm a fairy! Wizard's magic doesn't work on us."

"Can we go back now?" asked Liam.

"Not quite yet. Come join us!" Moonbeam called to Mertice.

"Did you see what the wizard did to the finch?" Annie asked Liam. "The poor little thing."

"Do you mean this little bird?" Moonbeam asked, reaching into her pocket. Raising the limp finch to her lips, she kissed the bird on her beak. The finch lifted her head and blinked at Moonbeam.

Annie gasped and Liam looked amazed. Moonbeam laughed. "Don't look so surprised. She was stunned, not dead. I felt her heart beating when I picked her up."

"I'm so glad!" said Annie.

The finch turned her head at the sound of Annie's voice. "I saved your life, didn't I?"

"You certainly did!" said Annie.

"And you saved my life," the finch said, turning back to Moonbeam. "Then I must stay with you until I have done the same for you."

Moonbeam looked delighted. "I would love to have you live with me! You'll really like my garden! Ah, there you are," she said, seeing Mertice. Once more the fairy raised her wand and pointed it at the wizard. With a light tap, the end of the sleeve that covered his mouth fell away, although his arms and hands were still bound.

"I hate what you've done to me, you crazy old fairy," the wizard shouted. "It makes me furious when anyone's magic is stronger than mine."

"Don't speak until you're spoken to, or I'll close your mouth permanently." Turning to Mertice, Moonbeam told her, "The wizard has to speak the truth now. Ask him anything you want."

"Are you a good man?" asked Mertice.

The wizard tried to keep his mouth closed, but the struggle didn't last long. "That depends on what you mean by good," he finally blurted out. "I'm good at getting what I want. I'm good at making people do as I say."

"Are you a cruel man?" Annie asked.

"Every chance I get," the wizard said with a pained expression on his face.

"Are you the man I thought you were?" the king said, staring intently at the wizard.

The struggle not to speak lasted longer this time, but finally the wizard's lips parted and the words tumbled out. "No. I never have been. I lied to you from the day we met."

"Then our agreement is null and void," said the king. Turning away from the wizard, he looked at each of the others in turn. "Thank you for opening my eyes. All of you. Now, if you'll take us back, I'll accompany my army home and see that my former wizard is locked away where he can't harm anyone ever again."

"Does that mean the siege is over?" asked Annie.

"Of course. I came here only because I believed his lies. He told me that my daughter had been kidnapped. A week ago an informant of his said that Mertice had been taken to Treecrest and held prisoner in the royal castle. I am sorry for believing him and hope that you will forgive me for all the trouble I have caused you. Mertice, I hope that you will join me. My fleet is waiting on the coast."

"I'd be happy to go home with you, Father," his daughter replied.

"By the way," he told Liam. "I met your brother. He had some sort of arrangement with my wizard."

"I know," said Liam. "Annie and I already took care of it."

"Then we must be off. Mertice and I have a lot of catching up to do."

"And Liam and I have to see about a wedding," Annie said, linking her arm with Liam's.

CHAPTER 17

THE FAIRIES WERE determined that the wedding was going to be the most beautiful one anyone had ever seen. They felt awful about what they had done, and had all decided that putting on the perfect wedding was the only way they could make up for it. By the time Annie, Liam, and Moonbeam returned to the castle, the fairies' preparations were well under way.

Annie was surprised to learn that her wedding was going to be that very night. When she offered to help, or at least give her opinion, Sweetness N Light shooed her away, saying, "I've already told your mother, your sister, and your friends that we don't need any help or interference. Go away and don't come back until I tell you we're ready."

"But—" Annie began.

"No buts about it! No one can put on a better wedding than a fairy, and you have every fairy in the kingdom working on this. Like I already said, go away!"

Annie walked off, feeling slightly stunned. She was finally about to get married! A hair tickled her neck and she brushed it back only to notice how grimy it felt. Suddenly all she could think of was a good, hot bath and clean clothes. On the way up the stairs, she stopped a maid and told her that she needed hot water. Only minutes after she reached her room, servants lugged in the tub while others carried in steaming buckets. Before they left, she had them move her dressing screen to block the magic mirror's view and ignored the face's grumbling.

When everyone was gone, Annie disrobed and climbed into the tub, letting the hot water ease her aching muscles. After washing her hair, she scrubbed herself until her skin was as clean as she could get it. She let her thoughts drift as she settled back in the still warm water, and found herself remembering the night before the failed wedding. Something niggled at her mind—something that had happened halfway through the night. When she remembered it, she sat up suddenly, making the water slosh back and forth.

"Magic mirror, did you say something to me the night before my wedding?"

She waited impatiently for a reply as the face took form on the other side of the screen. "What?" it finally said. "No 'Hello, mirror. How have you been while I was away, leaving you shut in a room with no company for days on end?'"

Annie sighed. "Hello, mirror, I'm sorry I left you alone for so long. Now will you answer my question?"

"I can't," said the mirror. "I said lots of things that night. You'll have to be more specific."

Annie reached for a towel and stepped out of the tub to dry herself. Slipping on a robe, she walked around the screen to face the magic mirror. "You woke me in the middle of the night and said something. What was it that you said?"

"I don't remember," the face said, looking irritable.

"Don't play games with me, mirror. You remember everything," said Annie.

"Why should I tell you?" the mirror asked. "You were rude and wouldn't talk to me."

"I was asleep and you woke me! I can't be held responsible for things I say when I'm still half-asleep. If you don't tell me right now, I'm going to sing!"

"You wouldn't!" said the mirror.

Knowing that the mirror hated her singing more than anything, Annie opened her mouth and started a song she had made up when she was little and her sister had once again refused to play with her. It was a short song, but it was filled with all the things she had loved as a child.

Unicorns with silver horns
Daisy chains to wear

"No!" shouted the face in the mirror. "Stop!"
"Then tell me what you said," Annie told him.

"I said that I knew something you didn't. There, are you satisfied?"

"Not until you tell me *what* you knew that I didn't." When the mirror didn't answer right away, Annie began to sing again.

Pennants snapping in a breeze,
Flowers in my hair

"Stop! All right! I'll tell you. I'd learned that the sprite wasn't really here to help you. He wanted to ruin your wedding because he said you'd ruined his life."

"Why didn't you tell me sooner? At least then we could have been a little more prepared."

"Because he didn't say it out loud until that night. I can't read people's thoughts, you know," said the mirror.

"So he said something the night before my wedding?" Annie asked.

The face in the mirror nodded. "All his plans were coming together and he was very pleased with himself. He sang a little song and danced a little dance. It was actually very entertaining."

"Is there anything else I should know?"

"Yes. You really do need to learn a better song. It sounds like a six-year-old wrote it."

"I believe I was five at the time," said Annie.

"See! Definitely time for a new song. Maybe one that isn't so happy!"

Annie turned away as the image faded from the mirror. As she dressed, she wondered what she should do until the wedding. Liam had already gone to retrieve Otis and Hunter, so there was no one she really wanted to see. Although she'd promised to answer questions, she wasn't in the mood to do it, so she decided to check how the fairies' repair work had gone. Hoping no one would find her, she took a little-used staircase to the upper floors to inspect the leaky roofs. From what she could see, all the water damage had been fixed, the floors and walls cleaned, and the ceiling looked new. She didn't see any sign that bats and squirrels had ever been there.

It was dusk when she headed to the kitchen to make sure the cooks had enough food, but she smelled the aroma of roasted ox and pheasant before she reached it. Changing direction, she headed for her mother's garden to see how it had fared. She was crossing the courtyard when she spotted Liam coming out of the stable, back from his errand.

"Did you find the horses easily enough?" Annie asked.

Liam nodded. "They'd found a small clearing and were gorging themselves on grass, but they both seem happy to be back in a stall with a bucket of oats."

"I've been inspecting the fairies' handiwork," said Annie. "They did a marvelous job fixing everything they'd damaged. I have to admit, sometimes magic can be a good thing."

"I've always thought so," Liam said, pulling her into his arms. "Especially the kind of magic we have."

"And what's that?" asked Annie.

"A different kind of magic. This kind." Still holding her in his arms, he kissed her until she could barely stand. When he finally pulled back, he cleared his throat and said, "I thought I'd go study some of your father's maps and find a place for our grand tour. I'll choose a few places, but I want you to help me with the final decision."

Annie nodded, missing the warmth of his arms when he let her go and walked away. Once again she headed for her mother's garden. She was admiring the roses, wondering why the fairies hadn't used them to decorate the great hall, when Sweetness N Light found her.

"It's time for you to get ready!" the fairy trilled. Raising her wand, she tapped Annie on the top of her head . . . And nothing happened. "What's wrong with this thing?" she muttered, tapping her wand against the palm of her other hand.

"Um, it's not your wand, it's me, remember? Magic doesn't work around me."

"Aphid eggs! You're right. I had forgotten. Well then, we'll have to do it the old-fashioned way. Take your clothes off while I conjure up your gown."

The gardeners looked up with interest, turning away when they saw that Annie had noticed. "I'm not taking my clothes off here!" she told the fairy.

"Oh, all right!" Sweetness N Light said, sounding exasperated. "Meet me in your bedchamber and you can get dressed there. Hmm . . . We'll have to do something about your hair."

When the fairy disappeared in a haze of sparkles, Annie turned and ran. Avoiding the great hall, she took the closest stairs and ran through the corridors until she reached her own chamber. Moonbeam was already there waiting with dozens of flower fairies. A pale blue gown covered with silver embroidery was draped across her bed, sparkling in the light of the already lit candles.

"It's gorgeous!" Annie said, gently caressing the fabric.

"Moonbeam saw to your dress," said Sweetness N Light. "Apparently she remembered that magic doesn't work around you, because she had one hundred fairies do all that embroidery by hand."

"Oh, my!" Annie exclaimed.

"Now you can take off your old gown," said Moonbeam. "Fairies, help me lift this thing. It weighs more than a sleeping gargoyle, and I've moved my fair share of those."

Annie threw off her everyday gown as the tiny flower fairies struggled to lift the heavy garment into the air. Ducking, she slipped into the new gown, adjusting the long slashed sleeves lined with silver and the heavy, embroidered skirt. Although from a distance the embroidery looked like an intricate design, up close it was a series of detailed interlocking flowers and butterflies.

"And now for your hair," said Sweetness N Light. "Fairies, the brush!"

Annie braced herself as the fairies fluttered around her head, brushing her hair, arranging it around a silver circlet and tucking individual flowers into the curls. "Is Liam getting ready?" she finally thought to ask. "Do my parents know it's almost time?"

"Yes, yes, we've handled everything. There," Sweetness N Light said as she tucked one last blossom into place. "You're all set. Oh, good. There's a mirror. Step over here and see how you look."

Annie followed the fairy's directions, but stopped partway when she realized that Sweetness N Light was taking her to the magic mirror. Even before she spoke, the mist in the mirror swirled and the face formed. Annie was surprised. It was the first time she had ever seen the face smile.

"Ooh! A magic mirror!" said Sweetness N Light. "I've heard about those. I'm going to ask it a question and I bet I know the answer! Mirror, mirror on the wall. Who's the fairest maid of all?"

"If you mean which girl who cleans is the fairest at games, that would be Maeve in the kitchen. She never cheats at jacks. But if you mean who is the most beautiful girl in the kingdom, that would be the princess

Annabelle. No one is more beautiful than a bride on her wedding day, especially this one."

"That's so sweet!" exclaimed Sweetness N Light. "Come along, fairies, we must escort our lovely bride downstairs."

They had all turned away and were headed to the door when the mirror muttered, "I had to say it. If I hadn't, she might have started to sing again." Annie smiled, but she was the only one who seemed to have heard it.

Sweetness N Light stopped at the door. "Buttercup, go see if they're ready for the princess in the great hall." After the little flower fairy had zipped away, Sweetness N Light turned to Annie, saying, "We need to arrive at just the right time so you can make your grand entrance without having to wait. Ah, here she is now. What took you so long?"

"Sorry," the little fairy replied. "Moonbeam said to tell you that they'll be ready by the time the princess walks down all those stairs."

Annie didn't care if the fairies thought she was slow; she practically flew down the stairs, stopping only when she was standing outside the door of the great hall. Gwendolyn, Snow White, and Ella were already there, dressed as bridesmaids in silver-gray gowns with blue flowers in their hair. They all looked beautiful, but what was so gratifying was that they seemed to think she did as well. They all smiled and made appreciative sounds, but no one dared speak, for the great hall was full and the procession was about to begin.

Although she was at the end of the line, Annie was able to see some of the things the fairies had done to the hall. There were flowers everywhere, from the blooming cherry trees growing in the corners to the violets nestled among the rushes that covered the floor. Wisteria vines clung to the columns and spread across the walls, their blooms hanging like fragrant grapes overhead. Lilies and rosebushes grew beside the tables that had been pushed against the walls, their heady scents mingling with those of the wisteria and the cherry blossoms to create their own perfume. Annie could swear she saw butterflies fluttering around the flowers and hummingbirds like living jewels darting from one welcoming bloom to another.

Sweetness N Light was standing in the doorway. At her signal, a whole flock of nightingales began to sing just as Gwendolyn took the first step into the great hall. Annie followed her friends, but it wasn't until she entered the hall herself that she was able to see Liam waiting for her by the dais. A light mist filled the hall, and Annie gasped when she saw why. The fairies had created a rainbow at the far end of the room, placed so it would frame Annie and Liam.

Annie's eyes glistened with tears as she walked slowly up the aisle. It was the most beautiful wedding she had ever seen and far surpassed anything she could have done herself. She smiled at her guests, spotting Lizette and Grimsby, Rose Red and Yardley seated behind Liam's father, King Montague. All of the princes who had tried to kiss Gwendolyn awake when she had been cursed were there as well, smiling back at Annie. Even Prince Digby, Gwendolyn's first suitor, seemed to be in a cheerful mood.

The fairies had done even more than she could have imagined. Any shred of resentment for their former mischief vanished, replaced by delight in what they had ultimately done. And then her eyes met Liam's as she stepped up beside him and she realized that the very best part of the wedding had been with her all along. As long as she had Liam, the rest was all just decoration.

With Liam at her side, gazing into her eyes, the wedding seemed to fly by in a beautiful blur. Before Annie knew it, the local priest was declaring them husband and wife and they were turning to face their family and friends. Suddenly dozens of white doves shot out of large woven-reed baskets to fly in a swirling loop overhead, then out the open windows. The nightingales began to sing again, and Annie saw more than one person dab tears from their eyes.

Within minutes Annie and Liam were standing alongside the bridesmaids and her parents in a formal receiving line. Her uncle and aunt, King Daneel and Queen Theodora, were the first to congratulate the bridal couple, along with Annie's cousin, Prince Ainsley.

Moonbeam was the next in line. "I have to say, this was the most fun I've had in ages! Oh, I know you said that helping your friend Mertice would be your wedding gift, but I just couldn't help myself. I had to make that gown because I knew exactly what you needed to wear, my dear. And I was right! It looks perfect on you. The only catch is, you're going to turn into a pumpkin at midnight. Just kidding!" she exclaimed when she saw the horrified look on Annie's face. "A little fairy godmother humor!"

Although Annie laughed, it wasn't very convincing. Magic didn't work on her, but even so . . .

"Are you happy, my dears?" Sweetness N Light asked, stepping in front of Annie and Liam. She peered into their eyes as if their answers were of vital importance.

"Very happy," Liam said, squeezing Annie's hand. "Thank you for all you've done."

Annie remembered how important appearing to be happy was to Sweetness N Light. She demanded that all the fairies in her garden be happy, and made their lives miserable if they didn't act like it.

"Yes," Annie said, glancing at Liam. "I've never been happier."

And it was the truth.